THE JUDAS METAL

Pat Williams and Robson Hyde were a successful partnership: they'd gained control of a silver mine down in south-west Texas, but when bandits began to ambush the loads of silver bullion, things changed. It appeared that the bandits had inside information. Who was behind the attacks? A resentful enemy sowed the seeds of doubt in Williams' mind. Did Hyde want all the silver for himself? Suspicion severely tested the pair's friendship, amid several violent deaths at the silver mine.

Books by Gillian F. Taylor
in the Linford Western Library:

DARROW'S LAW
CULLEN'S QUEST
SAN FELIPE GUNS
DARROW'S WORD
HYDE'S HONOUR
DARROW'S BADGE
TWO-GUN TROUBLE
SILVER EXPRESS

GILLIAN F. TAYLOR

$\blacklozenge$

THE JUDAS METAL

Complete and Unabridged

LINFORD
Leicester

First published in Great Britain in 2010 by
Robert Hale Limited
London

First Linford Edition
published 2011
by arrangement with
Robert Hale Limited
London

British Library CIP Data

Taylor, Gillian F.
    The Judas metal.- -(Linford western stories)
    1. Western stories.
    2. Large type books.
    I. Title II. Series
    823.9'14--dc22

    ISBN 978-1-44480-553-6

Published by
F. A. Thorpe (Publishing)
Anstey, Leicestershire

Set by Words & Graphics Ltd.
Anstey, Leicestershire
Printed and bound in Great Britain by
T. J. International Ltd., Padstow, Cornwall

This book is printed on acid-free paper

1

As the finishing touch Ramon Morales put his hat on carefully and scrutinized his reflection in the mirror. The crown of the black hat was an inch deeper than was usually worn by *criollo* gentlemen, and added subtly to his height. Ramon wasn't short, in fact he was a very average sort of height, but he liked to give the impression of being a little taller than he was. He always wore high-heeled riding boots, which had soles half an inch thicker than usual, and he always stood or sat with a straight back and his head up. As he looked in the mirror, he was pleased by what he saw.

His dark red *calzoneras* were tightly fitted around his slim hips and waist, set off with a yellow sash. Below the knee the trousers unbuttoned to flare out over his well-polished boots. Ramon's *calzoneras* were less exaggerated than was usual; this, with the narrow gold stripe that ran down the outer seams of the legs, helped to make him look taller. His short black jacket was trimmed with gold piping, to match the trim on his trousers, and the red-and-gold waistcoat he wore. Peering more closely at the mirror, Ramon inspected his neatly trimmed moustache and short goatee. Everything was just so. It was time to go and join Don Pedro and his daughter as they greeted the guests arriving for this very special *fiesta*.

It was nearly two years since Ramon Morales had last stayed at Don Pedro's hacienda, the Casa de las Flores. His mother was a cousin of Don Pedro's late wife, and they had visited regularly when he was a child. Now, as he walked briskly through the old building, he looked anew at the furnishings and decorations. It was as he remembered, a beautiful old house in the classic Spanish style. Everything about it suggested wealth and comfort. His father had owned a house like this, though smaller, until Texan settlers had claimed the land fifteen years ago. Ramon scowled to himself at the memory of that injustice. He wanted to talk to Don Pedro, to find out how the older man had managed to hold on to his large estates. There might be some kind of legal precedent he could use in the court case he was planning. Now, however, was not the time to think of such things.

Ramon stepped out of the cool adobe house and on to the porch, blinking briefly as his eyes adjusted to the bright April sunshine. He could hear the chatter of guests who had already arrived, and the distant strains of a solitary guitar. Already the smell of roasting meat was in the air, mingling with the scent of flowers. Beyond the sturdy adobe wall that surrounded the hacienda and its buildings was the dry land of the far south-western corner of Texas. Inside the walls were beds and tubs of the bright flowers that gave the

Casa de las Flores its name. And coming towards Ramon now was the sweetest and loveliest flower of them all.

Concepción Maria Flores de la Valle was just eighteen, a bright-eyed, sweet-faced girl. Ramon couldn't help smiling as he saw her; she was almost everything that a well-bred Spanish girl should be. Concepción was pretty, charming and excellent company. Her mother had died ten years previously, and the girl had the confidence of a woman used to hosting grand *fiestas* and running the household. At the moment though, Ramon thought she seemed both excited and nervous, looking to her father for reassurance.

Don Pedro de la Valle was a burly man with ponderous jowls and broad shoulders. He had a natural dignity, aided by his thick, greying hair and careful, deliberate movements. Just now, he was smiling benevolently at his daughter, but Ramon knew there was a shrewd mind behind the calm, patrician appearance. The young man studied the father and daughter as they approached the front steps of the house where he stood. For years Ramon had admired Don Pedro, and had taken him as an example of the traditional way of living. And now Don Pedro was about to use his daughter to betray everything Ramon had believed about him.

Ramon stepped forward, greeting Don Pedro and Concepción politely.

'*Buenos tardes, Don Pedro, Concepción*.' He continued, speaking in Spanish: 'Are you excited or nervous, Conchita?' He teased her gently, using the family pet-name for the girl.

'I'm excited about today,' she answered, speaking rapidly in their native language. 'But Pat and his family will be here any moment and I do hope his mother will like me.' She gazed at her father for reassurance.

Don Pedro smiled down at her. 'A good man like Pat Williams will have a good family, Conchita.'

Voices raised in greeting at the gates of the hacienda preceded the sound of hoofs and the rumble of wheels approaching. Concepción drew a little closer to her father, turning from Ramon to look where a rider and a carriage were entering the area in front of the main house. There were three women in the carriage, clearly a mother and her daughters. The two younger women were just a little older than Concepción, pretty, and bright with curiosity as they looked around at the grounds of the hacienda. Ramon spared them only a brief glance, however, studying the man riding alongside the carriage. He wasn't looking at the flowers though; his gaze was only for Concepción.

This was Pat Williams; a man with a half-share of a silver mine, and the *Anglo* who was to marry Concepción Maria Flores de la Valle. Ramon saw an honest-looking, slightly paunchy man, wearing a good-quality town suit. He noted that Williams sat his bay horse well, but he didn't look as though he'd be too dangerous with the short-barrelled gun worn in a rather shabby gunbelt. When Williams dismounted, landing more lightly than Ramon would have expected for a man of his build, the buckle of the gunbelt became more easily visible. Ramon recognized it immediately as a Confederate States Army buckle, and recalled Concepción's proud tales of how Williams and his mining partner had fought the Comanches. As Williams came closer, Ramon gauged the other man's height carefully, and saw that they were inch for inch the same. Without even thinking about it, Ramon straightened his back and raised his chin.

Ramon stayed in the background, silently watching Pat Williams as he introduced his mother and his sisters to Don Pedro and Concepción. Mrs Williams had a round face, with blue eyes that were charmingly merry in spite of the lines around them, and a good sprinkling of grey in her pale, reddish hair. Her dress, like those of her daughters, was obviously new and in the latest *Anglo* style. She smiled warmly at Concepción as the girl was introduced.

'Sure, an' I'm delighted to be meeting you at last,' Mrs Williams said, in her soft brogue. She held out both gloved hands to Concepción, who took them. 'It's wonderful to be having another daughter.'

The words went straight to Concepción's heart. 'I promise to be a good daughter to you,' she said impulsively. She spoke English well, but with a lilt that added to her charm. 'Please, call me Conchita.'

'Very well, Conchita. These are your sisters, Caitlin and Queenie.'

Caitlin was a younger version of her mother, but for her eyes. Her eyes were less contented. She studied Conchita's yellow dress and her jewellery, and unconsciously fluffed up the ruffles on her own pink gown. As the introductions were made, Caitlin's attention frequently wandered from the conversation to her surroundings. Ramon found her looking straight at him, assessing him in an open way he'd never experienced from a Spanish girl. He stared back at her, making her drop her eyes and look away.

Ramon was surprised when Queenie was introduced as the younger of the sisters, for she seemed to be the more mature. She was almost as tall as her brother, and had a graceful, slender figure. Even the shade cast by her parasol couldn't diminish the warm flame of the orange-red hair that burned even brighter against her cool, porcelain skin. At first glance, she seemed to Ramon like an exquisite sculpture, but when she was introduced to Conchita, Queenie's face lit up and her eyes sparkled like her mother's. Her dress was less fussy than Caitlin's, and she gave proper attention to the people she was meeting.

Concepción suddenly remembered her cousin's presence, and turned to him, urging him forward to be introduced. Ramon complied, keeping his expression bland as he came face to face with Pat Williams.

'This is Ramon Morales, one of my cousins,' Concepción explained, glancing at him before turning her gaze back to Williams. 'He's staying here for a while.'

'I'm pleased to meet you,' Williams said politely, holding out his hand.

Ramon wanted to answer in Spanish, the language that ought to be the only one heard at the Casa de las Flores, to see how Williams would react. However, he was all too aware of Don Pedro's formidable presence. Hiding his feelings, Ramon shook hands with Williams and greeted him politely in good English. Williams's grip was strong, and his palm felt hard, almost like a labourer's. After making his greeting, and bowing his head politely to the women, Ramon let Conchita take over the conversation again, and stayed behind as the group moved on.

Don Pedro was pointing out the different areas of the hacienda to

Caitlin and Queenie, while Conchita was talking to Pat Williams and his mother. Ramon allowed himself to brood over Williams. This ordinary-looking Texan, of undistinguished Irish descent, was the man Don Pedro thought most fit for his daughter. This was the man who would in time become owner and master of the Casa de las Flores. Ramon unconsciously ground his teeth in frustration as he thought of the end of an old way of life. Once again, the *Anglo* Texans were stealing the rightful heritage of the Mexicans. Ramon gave a sharp sigh of frustration, and headed off to look for his friend, Lorenzo Vargas. Lorenzo didn't like *Anglos* either, and could be relied on to listen sympathetically.

★ ★ ★

Pat Williams was too much engaged in the present to be thinking about the past or the future. Seeing the way his mother and Conchita took to one

11

another had taken a weight off his shoulders. With that worry resolved, and a cool drink of chia to take the dust from his throat, he was ready to enjoy the festivities. Conchita had suggested that they ride out to watch the riding and roping contests being held on the range close outside the hacienda walls. Fifty or so longhorns had been gathered in a restless, bellowing bunch, held together by *vaqueros* on their agile little horses. Dust rose around the whirl of movement, shot through now and again with glittering rays of sunlight reflected from the silver decorations the *vaqueros* wore on their clothes and on their horses' trappings. Some men were engaged in cutting single steers from the herd, while others twisted their horses back and forth, keeping the rest of the cattle together. When a steer was edged clear and started to run, a single *vaquero* would give chase, seizing the chance to show off his roping skills. Every catch brought cheers from the spectators, who were watching from a safe distance.

'I didn't reckon there'd be so many folks here!' Caitlin exclaimed, looking to a group further along the low ridge. Children ran around, a guitar and a violin played and the men and women smoked thin cigarettes and chattered as they watched the roping. 'Will they all be staying at the hacienda?'

Concepción answered her. 'It is most likely. Many of them work and live here. Others are friends and family who will find a space somewhere.'

'It's the biggest engagement party I ever saw,' Williams remarked, smiling down at Conchita.

She tilted her face up to look at him, for though he was of average height, her head barely came higher than his shoulder. 'Just wait until our wedding. The *fiesta* will last for a week.'

Williams switched to Spanish and told her, 'When I look at you, there is always a *fiesta* in my heart.'

Conchita's olive skin flushed a little and she smiled radiantly at him. Mrs Williams chuckled fondly at them. 'So that's how you won your pretty sweetheart,' she teased. 'Sure an' you used that good Irish blarney on her.'

Williams had forgotten that his mother and sisters spoke some Spanish too. He tried to cover his momentary embarrassment by glancing at the roping display. One of the *vaqueros* was riding towards them, but Williams's attention was drawn back to his family.

Concepción was pointing out some of the guests who were talking to her father a short distance away. Williams had met them at previous *fiestas*, and had been bored rigid by some of the older men. He grinned delightedly at Conchita's merciless description of her more tedious relatives.

'You-all look like you're having a swell time.'

Williams turned around at the familiar, languid South Carolina drawl, but his greeting trailed away into a sputter. He gawped at the *vaquero* in front of him for a moment, then laughter from Conchita and from Hyde told him that he'd been set up for a joke.

'You son-of-a . . . ' Williams bit off the words and contented himself with shaking his fist at his partner.

'You looked like you just saw a two-headed dog.' Hyde chuckled, his grey eyes bright with amusement.

Williams snorted and stepped back a pace to look his partner over. 'I bet you'd have been a nine-days wonder iffen you'd showed up to a plantation barbecue dressed like that,' he remarked.

Hyde was wearing a white shirt, a yellow bandanna, and the plain black jacket he usually favoured. His black boots and the double gunbelt with the ivory-gripped Colts were the same as ever, but he was wearing dark green *calzoneras* decorated with silver conchos along the outer leg, topped with a yellow sash. The two men had been partners for nearly a year, but

Williams had never seen Hyde wear anything so flamboyant before.

'Why've you gone all native?' Williams asked.

Hyde was starting to look a little self-conscious. 'I'm taking part in the roping contests. It seemed like a good idea at the time.'

Concepción spoke up. 'I think Señor Hyde looks fine.'

Williams grunted: he wasn't about to say so out loud, but the Mexican trousers suited Hyde's tall, slim-waisted build. The Southerner was a gentleman born and raised, and he wore the stylish clothes as well as any of the wealthy *criollos* present. Williams still had an occasional twinge of jealousy over how readily Don Pedro and his contemporaries had accepted Hyde as one like themselves. Then he felt Conchita's arm brush against his, and looked at her sweet face. His natural good-humour rapidly asserted itself, and he began introducing Hyde to his mother and sisters.

Mrs Williams gave Hyde a warm,

motherly smile and promptly invited him to come and eat with the family whenever he liked. Caitlin smiled brightly, giggled and tilted her head to one side as she looked up at him.

'Pat's told us a lot about you,' she said enthusiastically, causing Hyde to give Williams a dark look. In contrast to Caitlin, Queenie seemed almost shy. She and Hyde looked wonderingly at one another until the colour suddenly rose in her cheeks and she looked away.

'I'm real pleased to meet you,' she said simply.

'I'm honoured,' Hyde answered, still looking at her. After a few moments, he broke his gaze and turned away sharply. 'It's about my turn for some roping. I just came by to be sociable for a minute,' he added, showing a sudden, sharklike grin to Williams.

'Go out there and show us you can rope like a *vaquero* better than you dress like one,' Williams told him, watching as Hyde mounted a little buckskin horse that carried the hacienda's brand. Hyde waved to them, then jogged his horse down the slope to the milling herd.

'I hope he'll be all right,' Queenie said, watching him ride away. 'Those cows look pretty wild.'

'He said he'd rode a couple of spells with beef outfits,' Williams answered. 'And Hyde's plumb good at looking after himself.' He didn't add that he'd never actually seen Hyde rope a steer, but he knew his partner was good at almost every physical skill he turned his hand to.

A few minutes later they got to see if Williams's confidence was justified. A black-and-white steer was cut out of the mob, and the buckskin horse took off after it. The horse knew its job, closing in of its own accord, while Hyde shook out a loop and swung his rope. The steer and the horse pounded flat out across the ground as Hyde made his throw. Williams held his breath as the loop flew through the air, then let it out in a whoop as the rope settled around the steer's six-foot spread of horns. The buckskin horse stopped dead as Hyde rapidly dallied the rope around the saddle horn. Horse and rider braced themselves as the steer hit the end of the rope at full gallop. Its head jerked and it crashed to the ground in a cloud of dust.

'I said he'd be just fine,' Williams crowed triumphantly.

The black-and-white steer scrambled to its feet almost immediately, apparently unhurt. It bellowed, then charged straight at the horse and rider. Hyde held his horse in place as the steer charged with its head lowered and the lethal horns aimed forward. The steer was barely ten yards away when the buckskin jumped aside and backed up. Hyde barely shifted in the saddle as the horse leapt about beneath him. His hands were on the rope and his attention was on the steer as it spun around almost in its own body length, and repeatedly charged him. The watchers were so engrossed in the battle that they never saw exactly what started the stampede.

2

The mob of steers was suddenly on the move, a mass of horns and tails pounding along in a solid block. The *vaqueros* yelled, urging their horses after the stampeding cattle. Hyde heard the sudden drumming of hoofs and glanced over his shoulder, seeing the herd heading straight for him. As he looked at the cows, the steer charged him again, and the buckskin horse twisted out of the way. Williams gasped as Hyde lurched in the saddle at the unexpected move. With his attention on maintaining his seat, Hyde couldn't work his rope properly. As the horse and the steer turned around one another, the rope caught behind the steer's hind legs. Its head jerked back and its back legs lifted, flipping it over in a violent, corkscrew somersault. The steer's neck snapped as it hit the ground and it lay in a solid, immobile mass.

The buckskin horse lunged forwards, trying to flee from the stampede. The dead weight of the steer on the end of the rope brought it up short. It stopped almost as suddenly as the steer had, pulled clean off its feet. Williams swore and one of the women screamed as Hyde and his horse hit the ground.

'Get up!' Williams yelled futilely. He felt sick, too far away to be of any help to his friend.

Hyde rolled and came up on to his feet. The buckskin was snorting with fear, its eyes rolling as it struggled to get to its legs. Hyde jumped for his horse, throwing himself across the saddle, and seizing the pommel with his left hand as he drew his revolver with his right. He fired once as the horse lurched upright. The rope parted and the buckskin staggered for a moment. Hyde hauled himself astride his saddle and grabbed for the dangling reins. The horse leapt straight into a gallop as the mob of cattle surged up to it. A rolling cloud of dust, beaten from the dry ground by the herd's hoofs, covered the scene.

'Pat! Is he all right?'

Williams hardly knew who had asked the question. He was peering down the slope to the stampeding mob, his hands clenched into fists as he tried to see what was happening. Conchita was clutching his arm, muttering prayers under her breath.

'There he is!' It was Queenie's clear voice. 'He's safe!'

Williams's heart leapt as he made out the familiar figure, half-visible in the dust cloud at the edge of the charging herd. Hyde was riding alongside the leaders, defying the tossing horns to slap his hat against the face of the nearest steer. It veered away from him, pushing those beside it to the right. Hyde kept his place, riding right alongside the pounding mob of cattle, working with the vaqueros to turn the herd. Under pressure from the riders, the herd began to circle.

'They've got it now,' Williams said thankfully.

'Thanks be to God,' his mother said, crossing herself.

'Amen,' answered Queenie. Like the others, she was watching intently, but her attention wasn't on the grand spectacle of the herd circling in on itself. Her eyes were only for the tall rider on the buckskin horse.

★　★　★

In the evening the festivities turned to dancing on the big patio of the hacienda. Almost everyone, from Don Pedro to the families of the *vaqueros*, danced at least once in the evening. The air was warm with the smell of barbecued food, and lively with conversation, music and laughter. Hyde was enjoying himself amongst the dancers, refreshed by good food and a wash and brush-up after his earlier adventures at roping. As one tune finished, he bowed to his partner and excused himself, in passable, if poorly accented, Spanish as he needed to take a drink.

His glass was on the table where Pat Williams and his family were sitting. Mrs Williams smiled at him as he finished his glass of wine.

'You dance well,' she said. 'I guess you've taken no real hurt from coming off your horse this afternoon?'

'Why, a few bruises here and there,' Hyde drawled. 'Nothing to worry none about.' His attention was caught by the announcement of the next dance. It was of the sort he had been waiting for: a set dance that had regular changes of partner. Hyde bowed to Caitlin.

'I'd sure be honoured if you'd dance this with me, Miss Caitlin?'

'I'd love to,' she answered eagerly, and stood up so fast her chair almost fell over backwards. Caitlin continued talking as Hyde took her to join the other dancers.

'I was never at such a large dance before,' she said, glancing around at the other people. 'And such lovely clothes. I hope my dress is all right,' she added, shaking up the ruffles on the wide skirt.

'It looks fine to me, but I'm no expert on ladies' fashions,' Hyde answered.

'You must have seen balls and parties as fancy as this before the war,' Caitlin went on. 'Pat used to mention you when he wrote us, especially when he told us that he'd done asked you to be a full partner in the mine. He said how your family used to own a big plantation in South Carolina, and that you were a for-real gentleman.'

'My mammy done her best at making me a gentleman,' Hyde answered coolly. He took his place opposite Caitlin and took her hands, ready for the dance.

'I bet those dances must have been glorious,' Caitlin went on. 'All the women in those fine dresses — silks and muslins and taffetas. Everything elegant and stylish, in a big, lovely house.'

'It was a good time iffen you were rich,' Hyde answered shortly. He was relieved to hear the music begin, and began to guide Caitlin through the first steps of the dance. She was too busy concentrating on the dance to keep talking about the past, and forcing him to relive bitter-sweet memories.

As Hyde had known, the pattern of the dance meant that he only spent part of the time actually dancing with Caitlin. He glanced at her now and again as he turned and circled with other ladies. She was smiling at all her partners, enjoying the novelty of meeting so many men so quickly. They finished the dance together, then Hyde took her back to the table.

'That was delightful, thank you so much,' Caitlin said, lingering by his side.

He barely heard her as he took a quick drink of his red wine. All through the last dance he'd been stealing looks towards the table. Queenie had remained there, sitting quietly beside her mother as they watched the dancing. Now was the time he'd really been waiting for. A quiet word and a few dollars given to the leader of the musicians earlier meant that the next dance would be a slow, stately one. He'd danced first with Caitlin, the elder sister. Now Hyde summoned his courage and looked across the table to Queenie. She was watching him steadily with her wide, green eyes, in a way that somehow gave him confidence. He asked her to dance.

Once he was among the other dancers, with Queenie's hand in his, Hyde began to relax a little.

'Have you settled into your new house yet?' he asked.

Queenie smiled and nodded. 'It's a lovely place Pat's got for us in Hueco. It sure seems like luxury, having a room to myself after sharing all my life.' They began dancing slowly, circling round one another in the formal steps of the dance.

'A little town like Hueco must seem quiet after San Antonio,' Hyde said.

'It's big enough for me,' Queenie replied, looking up with a smile that almost took his breath away. 'And it's good to be seeing Pat again, though I kind of miss Felicity.' Hyde nodded to show he understood who she meant. Felicity was the eldest of Pat Williams's three sisters. She'd worked as a school-teacher to help support the family while Pat had searched for the mine their father had found. Now that the mine was producing Felicity had married and stayed behind in San Antonio, while the other women came to join Pat out near the silver mine.

'I'd like to see my mother and my sister again sometime,' Hyde told Queenie, surprising himself with the sudden confession. 'I write them more often now I can send money back regular, but I haven't seen them in near on four years.'

Queenie looked at him with a warm steadiness that reassured him. There was something about her; a kind of serenity, but stronger. Hyde's first impression of her had been of beauty, of the glowing red-orange hair, jade-green eyes and por-celain skin. Then, when they'd looked deeply at one another, he'd got the feel-ing of constancy within her; this was a woman he could draw strength from.

'I guess your family should be proud of you,' Queenie said. The movements of the dance brought them face to face, barely a hand's-breadth apart. Then they stepped back and away.

'I aim for them to be proud of me,' Hyde answered her. He'd come close to disgracing himself and losing his honour, not too long ago, and the subject made him uncomfortable. He didn't want anything to spoil the pleasure of dancing with Queenie. 'Pat said he was getting a horse for you.'

Queenie smiled. 'Yes, he promised to take me to the Schmidts' ranch sometime next week. I'm looking forward to being able to ride out and explore as much as I want.'

Hyde frowned slightly as he raised their joined hands for her to turn in a circle. 'This is still dangerous country. There's Comanche, Apache and ban-dits about, besides puma and bears. You won't be safe riding about on your own.'

'I guess you're right,' she said disappointedly. 'Pat did say I'd have to stay close to town.' They looked at one another, then both smiled.

'I'd be honoured to accompany you when you go riding,' Hyde said.

'I should like that,' Queenie answered. The words were simple, but her face told him so much more.

Hyde smiled, and saw her smile in return until the steps turned them away from one another for a few moments. As he turned, Hyde glimpsed Williams dancing with Concepción. He suddenly remembered that Queenie was his partner's sister, and felt a sudden unease at how Williams would react to their riding out together. Something must have shown in his face as he turned back to Queenie, for she gave him a puzzled look.

'I was wondering how Pat would feel iffen I said I wanted to go riding with his sister,' Hyde explained.

Queenie smiled confidently as she took his hand for an in-and-out step. 'For sure, I don't see why he would object.'

'For one thing, I'm thirteen years older than you.'

Queenie looked him full in the face, holding his gaze with her green eyes. 'That makes no difference to me.'

Hyde felt some of his earlier confidence returning. 'All the same, I don't reckon we should tell Pat anything just yet. He'll say how we've only just met, and that it's too soon to start courting.'

Queenie nodded. 'But if I want to go out riding next week, will you ride with me?'

There was only one answer in Hyde's heart. 'Yes.'

★   ★   ★

Ramon Morales had found himself a seat where he could watch Williams and his family without being too obvious. He had a bunch of grapes in front of him and was eating his way steadily through them. Ramon loved grapes, and usually ate them slowly, and with pleasure, but right now he was barely aware of what he was tasting. Beside him, Lorenzo Vargas blew a thin stream of cigarette smoke to the starry sky.

'The engagement is announced now,' Lorenzo remarked, in Spanish. 'You may as well stop sulking.'

Ramon tore another grape off the bunch. 'I do not like the idea of the Casa de las Flores becoming the property of an upstart Texan.' He thrust the grape into his mouth and bit into it fiercely.

'Concepción appears to love him, and Don Pedro approves,' Lorenzo remarked. 'I don't think you could get them both to change their minds.'

'I wish Pat Williams had never come to Hueco county.'

'He's here. You have to wish for him to leave.'

'To leave alone, and permanently,' Ramon added with emphasis. 'I would be happy if he were dead.'

'To kill an *Anglo* is not a sin,' Lorenzo said quietly.

Ramon turned to look at him. They were second cousins, and had known one another from childhood, growing up on similar *estancias*, though Lorenzo's family had kept their land after Ramon's family had lost theirs to settlers. Ramon was the elder by a couple of years, and, more importantly to him, an inch taller. Lorenzo had grown into a barrel-shaped man, with a powerful chest and shoulders. His build, and the way he looked at people, as though planning to challenge them, gave the impression of a man not to be trifled with. Ramon had seen for himself that this air of potential malice was for real. He studied his friend thoughtfully before replying.

'To kill an *Anglo* may not be a sin, but it is still a crime,' he replied. 'And Williams is a rich *Anglo* and he has important connections here now. The man who killed Williams would soon find himself on the end of a rope.'

Lorenzo nodded thoughtfully, and took a long draw on his cigarette. 'That is very likely,' he conceded, smoke trickling from his mouth as he spoke. 'If they were to catch the killer. Do you think the lawmen would be that good?'

Ramon turned to look at the table where Williams was sitting. 'The lawmen might not find a killer, but I think that Williams's friend, Hyde, would search long and hard to take his revenge. Hyde would be a bad man to cross.' He paused and thought for a moment. 'If Williams were to cross Hyde . . . ?'

Lorenzo had also turned and was looking at Williams's table. 'If Williams and Hyde were to fight, Hyde would win. They are both tough men, but Señor Hyde is very quick and good with his guns.'

'But would he kill his partner? Which of them has more to lose?' Ramon asked, his gaze intent on the two *Anglos*.

'I say Williams.'

Ramon picked another grape off the bunch and rolled it between thumb and fingers. 'They both have a share of the silver mine, but yes, Williams has a future as son-in-law to Don Pedro. He will have Concepción for his wife and this estate for his own. That is a lot for a man to lose.' He popped the grape into his mouth and chewed on it absent-mindedly. 'If Williams thought that Hyde was cheating him, that he was losing money from the mine and might lose Concepción, he would become desperate. He might be foolish enough to draw on Hyde, who would kill him in self-defence. And if Williams should be lucky enough to kill Hyde, who has done nothing wrong, then it would be Williams swinging at the end of a rope.'

Lorenzo chuckled. 'If we are really lucky, the *Anglos* will kill one another. But how do you convince a man that his partner is cheating him?'

'It will take time,' Ramon said

thoughtfully. 'The silver mine will be the key. Judas betrayed Jesus for silver, and Williams will betray himself, believing that Hyde has betrayed him.' He smiled.

3

Robson Hyde picked up the last month's receipts and arranged them by date order. He stacked the different-sized pieces of paper as neatly as possible, and put them on the desk beside the ledger. Taking up his pen, he dipped it in the cast-iron inkwell and began entering the details in a flowing, copperplate hand. It was fairly peaceful in the office of the Two Moccasins mine; the only real noise was from the pounding of the stamp mill further up the canyon, which Hyde barely noticed any more.

The office was the front half of a sturdy new adobe building near the entrance to the canyon. The back half was divided into two small bedrooms, where Hyde and Williams slept. Nearby was another new building, a lumber bunkhouse where the mine workers lived, and where everyone ate. Most of the furnishings were plain, even here in the office. The chairs were simply made and the desk was a pine table. Two pairs of buffalo horns fastened on to the wall served as a coat- and hat-rack, while a Mexican rug spread in front of the desk added a splash of colour. By far the most expensive-looking item in the room was the large safe. This was very new, decoratively finished, and fixed against the thick adobe wall.

Hyde worked peacefully for a while, bringing the books up to date. Williams had freely admitted that he struggled with accounting. He spent his time supervising the men, using his personal warmth to defuse arguments when necessary, and lending a hand at digging or sorting ore when needed. Hyde dealt with the money, made sure necessary supplies were available, and commanded the journey that took silver bullion from the mine to the bank in El Paso. He was willing to help out with most tasks around the mine when necessary, but he rarely ventured into the dark tunnel that led into the side of the canyon.

The sound of his horse whinnying a greeting caused Hyde to look up from his work. His riding-horse, Cob, was kept in a small corral close to the adobe. Hyde stood up and moved so he could see through the small window on the side of the building. Just visible beyond the willow trees that shaded the corral were three riders: Williams, Don Pedro and Concepción. Hyde returned to the desk in two quick strides, and slipped a sheet of blotting paper into the ledger before closing it. He could hear the visitors' voices outside as he collected his hat from the buffalo horns. His gunbelt hung there too, and Hyde was buckling it into place before he thought about what he was doing.

He paused, looking in the direction of the voices still on the other side of the door. This was the first time that Don Pedro or his daughter had visited the silver mine. Soon after Williams and

Hyde had arrived at the mine they had run into trouble with Marco de la Valle. Marco, Don Pedro's only son, had been a hot-headed young man, who had become obsessed with owning the silver mine. Marco had even gone so far as to recruit Comanches to do his dirty work in killing Williams and Hyde. His attempts had failed, and Hyde had been forced to shoot Marco in self-defence. Hyde knew that his killing of Don Pedro's son had been forgiven, but it couldn't be easily forgotten. As the months had passed, Hyde had grown easier about meeting Don Pedro, but the silver mine had uncomfortable associations for both of them. Hyde looked down at his gunbelt, and the ivory-handled Colts, then sternly banished thoughts of the past and went to deal with the present.

Pat Williams was standing beside Don Pedro, telling him about those of the buildings and structures that were visible. Concepción was bending over a tabby cat that lay on a crudely made bench in front of the office building. As she rubbed behind its torn ear, the rangy cat rolled on to its back and yawned.

'*Como se llamo?*' she asked Hyde, smiling with a hint of mischief.

'*Le gato se llama Tiger*,' he answered after a moment's hesitation.

Concepción laughed merrily. '*Bueno*! Your Spanish is improving but your accent is still dreadful.'

'It surely can't be as bad as my French accent,' he answered cheerfully, and turned to greet Don Pedro.

As they were talking, a gangly young man came up and took the horses' reins.

'*Gracias*, Balzar,' Hyde drawled.

Balzar smiled happily and led the horses away, his movements accompanied by the jingling of his fancy silver spurs. Don Pedro watched him leave, not quite concealing some concern. Although he'd never visited the mine before, he'd heard plenty about its people from what Williams had told

Concepción, and he knew that Balzar had a childlike mind, in spite of being twenty years old. Hyde saw the look of concern, and understood.

'Your horses will be just dandy with Balzar,' he said. 'I trust him completely with Cob.'

Don Pedro nodded, his heavy features lifting into a smile. 'I never saw a horse so well turned out as yours,' he answered politely. He turned to look around him, his piercing dark eyes taking in the cleared areas and the new buildings. 'I used to hunt here when I was a young man,' he remarked. 'This canyon looks very different now.'

'I guess it was a lot purtier then,' Hyde answered, falling into step alongside him as the group started walking. The tabby cat ran alongside them for a little way, then vanished into the bushes on business of his own.

'What's that building?' Concepción asked, pointing to the large lumber building next to the adobe office.

'That's the men's bunkhouse and

cookshack,' Williams told her.

'Oh.' Concepción darted quick glances at the windows as they passed. Curiosity over seeing the men's quarters warred against the knowledge that a young lady should stay well away from such places.

A little way beyond the bunkhouse was the tool shed, conveniently close to the mine entrance. Hyde found himself taking a deep breath as he followed the others into the tunnel in the side of the canyon.

'Watch where you're walking,' Williams warned the visitors. 'It's plumb easy to catch your foot on the rail ties.'

Lanterns hanging from timbers supporting the roof glinted light on the narrow rails that led away into the mine.

'The burro cars take the ore from down in the mine to the head of the mill,' Williams explained as he followed the rails further in.

'Doesn't the burro mind coming down here in the dark?' Concepción asked.

'She don't seem to,' Williams answered.

Hyde minded the dimly lit tunnels

and the roof of rock that ran so close above his head. He barely heard a word of Williams's talk or the distant noise from the men working further down the mine. His hearing was tuned to the slight sound of falling dirt; the first warning of a cave-in. Williams turned off from the main tunnel and took them down a narrow one where the ore had played out. The only light now was from the lantern that Williams had taken from the main tunnel. It was a mercifully short tunnel that lead to a dead end, like the one Hyde had been trapped in a few months before. He stood silently as Williams explained how the ore was dug, schooling his face into a stoic mask while his heart pounded heavily and his skin crawled with fear.

The fear stayed with him as they picked their way back along the narrow tunnel. It eased a little when they reached the main tunnel and Williams turned back to the distant glow of sunlight; then Concepción asked,

'Can't we go and see the faces being worked?'

Hyde's stomach tightened and the raw fear showed briefly on his face as he glanced down into the depths of the mine. Then Williams's answer began to sink in and he found he could breathe again.

'We'd best not go down there,' Williams was saying. 'It's real hot and sweaty work and the men find it easier iffen they take off some of their clothes.'

'They wouldn't like having a lady visit them when they're working,' Don Pedro added firmly.

Concepción resigned herself to missing the shocking delight of seeing men with their shirts off, and began to lead the way out. Hyde smothered a sigh of relief and saw Williams looking at him. There was sympathy in Williams's good-natured face, and Hyde knew that Williams had been thinking of more than protecting Concepción's modesty by not going deeper into the mine. That unstated support made the journey

45

back through the mine a great deal easier for Hyde.

Out in the sunshine again, he was able to join in the conversation as they toured the canyon. The rails led by the stamp mill, where the ore was sorted. Waste material was hauled over to the far side of the canyon and dumped on the pile of tailings. The ore-bearing rock was fed into the stamp mill, where iron plates crushed it to fine fragments.

'Most of the machinery here was set up before I took over,' Williams told Don Pedro and Concepción, speaking loudly to be heard above the din of the plates smashing the ore. 'When we've built up more capital, we aim to get a steam-powered mill and set it closer to the processing machinery.'

'We need to take a few more loads of bullion to the bank before we can do that though,' Hyde added.

He led them further upstream, to a quieter spot, where the big corral was. The corral was built across the bubbling creek, so the animals had a constant supply of water. Here were half a dozen saddle horses and three fine mules. A chestnut horse came over to them and pushed its muzzle between the rails, nickering hopefully for titbits. Concepción smiled and stroked the velvety skin around its nostrils.

'Half the horses belong to the miners,' Williams explained. 'The two greys and the bay roan belong to the mine. The mules do too.'

'We use them for packing bullion out to El Paso and hauling supplies back in,' Hyde added. 'There's a greater choice of routes if we use mules instead of a wagon. It makes it easier to keep out of sight from anyone who fancies getting their hands on our silver. I prefer to travel light and fast.'

'You speak as a soldier there,' Don Pedro remarked.

Hyde nodded and made a wry smile. 'Why, I might as well get some good out of that damned war. I learnt plenty about scouting and escorting supply trains, though I never dreamed I'd be escorting my own silver bullion one day.'

'*Our* silver,' Williams put in, his voice loud with mock indignation.

Hyde grinned at him, as Concepción giggled and Don Pedro smiled.

'Our silver,' Hyde agreed. 'Which means that half of it is mine.' He began walking back along the canyon.

'Half the profits, and half of any debt too,' Williams pointed out, falling into step alongside Concepción as they walked.

'Full partners,' said Hyde. 'As long as that seam holds out, anyhow.'

Concepción glanced from one man to the other. 'If I could marry both of you, I'd be living on all the money from the mine,' she said wickedly.

Williams took her arm possessively. 'You're already promised just to me, Conchita. Hyde can go find himself his own woman.'

'Maybe I'll do just that,' Hyde remarked.

Thoughts of Queenie occupied him

as they looked around the processing building. Here the crushed ore went into the large pans of the Washoe processor. The pans were covered, but Williams told his guests how the ore was mixed with water, salt, mercury and copper sulphate, then heated and agitated by the steam-powered machinery.

'Most miners have their own recipe,' he told them. 'McKindrick here is in charge of the processing and smelting.'

McKendrick was a black-haired Scot, clad in a collarless shirt and a faded kilt of green and red tartan that revealed his knotty calves and scarred knees. He was one of the first men whom Williams had hired, and had proved his worth as a foreman. Concepción was fascinated by his kilt, and by the black chest hair that poked out from the open neck of his shirt. She clearly didn't know quite where to look as McKindrick explained how the amalgam from the pans was smelted in the furnace to separate the silver from the mercury. The gleam of humour in McKindrick's dark eyes suggested that he'd noticed her dilemma, but he made no reference to it.

Leaving McKindrick to his alchemies, they stepped outside back into the spring sunshine.

'It has been a most interesting visit,' Don Pedro said, following Williams back towards the office building. 'I had never thought much about how metals are obtained from the rocks.'

'There's a sight more to it than I realized afore I started here,' Williams admitted, picking his way neatly across the stepping stones that spanned the creek. 'And silver's harder to extract than gold. It combines more readily with other minerals. We're losing some of the silver in the processing, but that's inevitable.'

'Then other mines have the same problem?' Don Pedro asked. 'Even the Comstock lode?'

Williams nodded. 'The Comstock ore is galena, which yields gold and silver, mostly silver. They had some trouble processing that properly.'

Concepción let the two men draw ahead as they talked about mining, turning her attention to Hyde.

'Visiting the mine reminded me of the caves that Marco and our cousins used to play in,' she remarked.

'Were they safe?' Hyde asked, without thinking.

Concepción nodded. 'There are natural caves to the north of our land. They are solid rock. The biggest risk was of the boys getting lost, if they went too far in. They would never let me go further than the entrance cave when we went there,' she added, with a becoming pout.

Hyde chuckled, distracted from thoughts of dark tunnels and rock falls by Concepción's playful childishness.

'Why, I'm sure you're the only one who's gotten to see a working silver mine,' he drawled. 'And there surely can't be many women who've seen the mine that produced the metal to make their engagement ring.'

Concepción smiled and laughed. Holding up her left hand, so the sun shone on her ring, she pirouetted around in an excess of high spirits. The full skirts of her dark red dress flared out and swung round with her light movements. She made a bright, enchanting picture, which drew the attention.

No one noticed the reappearance of the cat from the scrub, until it had almost reached Concepción. The rangy tabby trotted up to her, uttering the slightly muffled yowl of a cat with prey. Hyde glanced at the cat and felt a start of horror as he realized it was carrying a live snake in its mouth. The cat had caught the snake just behind its head and was dragging it along, as the snake hissed and thrashed. The end of its tail vibrated with a tell-tale buzz. As it reached Concepción, the tabby dropped the furious snake and jumped back. The rattler thrashed around, coiling itself up. Concepción let out a half-scream and froze as the snake raised its wide head in her direction. The rattler opened its mouth wide, the long upper fangs visible as it hissed angrily.

Hyde was some six feet away from Concepción and the snake. He drew almost without thinking but, in that split second of movement, kept cool enough to raise the gun to shoulder level for a more accurate shot. The Colt cracked and the snake's head was torn from its body. The cat leapt away and bolted into the juniper scrub. The snake's scaly body collapsed into a loose heap in front of Concepción. She blinked at it, took a sharp breath, and vented her feelings with a near-hysterical scream.

4

Pat Williams was the first to recover from the shock. He sprinted to Concepción and threw his arms around her, asking soft, anxious questions as she clung to him and shook. Don Pedro started towards them, then stopped, one hand reaching towards his frightened daughter. He watched Williams comforting her for a moment, then turned to Hyde. Don Pedro's dark eyes showed a warmth Hyde had rarely seen before. Don Pedro walked up to him, his movements as steady and deliberate as ever, in spite of the strong emotions in his heavy face. Hyde holstered his gun and took the hand that de la Valle offered.

'Señor Hyde.' Don Pedro paused to clear his throat.

'Anyone would have done the same.' Hyde put in, before Don Pedro could say more.

Don Pedro shook his head. 'Not everyone could have done the same as you. I am in your debt.'

Hyde felt a stab of guilt at the words. 'Maybe I just paid a debt,' he said quietly, thinking of Don Pedro's son.

'You killed Marco to save your own life, and Pat's. Pat Williams will be my son-in-law, and a good one. There is no debt.'

Hyde managed a shaky smile, and a knot in the back of his conscience finally began to unwind.

★   ★   ★

The story of the snake and Concepción's narrow escape was the talk of the hacienda for the next day or so. The story grew in the telling, until Hyde had been standing twenty feet away, instead of six, and the snake was a full-grown adult, far larger than any cat could drag. Concepción couldn't help feeling a little sorry that it hadn't been Pat who'd shot the snake so dramatically, but she was truly thankful to Hyde. She was somewhat surprised when her cousin, Ramon, criticized Hyde's actions.

He had joined her in the small, shady courtyard at the centre of the sprawling house. As usual, Ramon sat very straight in his chair; he never seemed to relax, or slump down as other people did. Concepción was sitting with her guitar on her lap, plucking soft notes now and again as they talked. She was quite fond of Ramon, in spite of his obsession about his height and his rather snobbish views. He was certainly one of the most handsome of her many cousins, and she liked his neat moustache and goatee better than the large moustaches worn by other young men she knew. Although he was ten years older than she was, Concepción remembered that he had been kind to her when she was a child, fetching her tit-bits from the kitchen and lifting her up to the saddle of his horse for a ride.

'I believe that Hyde took an unnecessary risk in shooting a snake like that.'

Ramon spoke in Spanish. 'If he had missed, the shot would certainly have provoked the snake into biting you. And you tell me how quickly he made the shot. What if it had gone wide and hit you? He must have known the risk of hitting you, instead of the snake.'

'But he did kill the snake,' Concepción protested. 'Hyde is a very fine gunman. He wasn't going to shoot me by mistake.'

Ramon shook his head. 'A man who is so good with his guns would know how dangerous a fast shot like that is. He was not so careful as he should have been. If the shot went well, he would be a hero. If it did not, you could get hurt, but he was willing to risk that.'

Concepción snorted inelegantly. 'Why would Señor Hyde take such a risk? He has no reason to want to risk hurting me.' She plucked a dissonant chord on the guitar.

Ramon took a deep breath and let it out slowly. 'You told me that Señor Hyde used to live like this.' He gestured at the house and the carefully tended plants in the courtyard. 'His family were wealthy landowners.'

'They had a rice plantation and, I think, a house in Charleston also.' Concepción wondered what Ramon was getting at.

'So he was used to owning land, a fine home and slaves, no doubt. He had good horses, fine clothes and slaves to look after him,' Ramon said. 'He went to war to protect all that, and fought for four years, but he lost everything. Now he comes here, to the Casa de las Flores, and he sees what he has lost. And he sees that Pat Williams will one day have all this, by marrying you. I think Hyde may be jealous of Williams having what he has lost.'

Concepción was momentarily lost for words, half-wondering whether Ramon was playing some kind of joke on her. There was no humour in his eyes though. She suddenly found her voice and leaned forward as she spoke to her cousin.

'You think Hyde would hurt me, or let me get hurt, because he is jealous of Pat? He is not interested in marrying me,' Concepción said, certain of herself on that point. 'And he has been a loyal friend to Pat. They have fought together, and worked together,' she continued passionately. 'Why, Pat trusts Hyde so much that it is Hyde who escorts the silver bullion from the mine to El Paso!'

Ramon held up one hand in a gesture of peace. 'Forgive me! I did not mean to upset you. I do not know these *Anglos* so well as you, Conchita. I was just thinking about why Hyde should have made a quick, risky shot like that.'

'He wanted to kill the rattlesnake and stop it from biting me.'

'Of course,' Ramon said soothingly. 'Most likely there is no more to it than that.' He paused, looking at Concepción in the way he had when she was a little girl, and he was explaining something to her. 'I still believe that Señor Hyde is a dangerous man. He is too quick to use his guns.'

Concepción shrugged. 'Like you said, he was a soldier. He volunteered at the start of the war and fought until the surrender. He needed to be quick with his guns to survive, as you know yourself,' she added. Concepción resisted the urge to say that Hyde had been a captain, and would have been promoted to major if pneumonia hadn't kept him in hospital when the rank needed to be filled.

Ramon had been keen on an army career, and had joined up in 1864. He'd returned to his family after the War Between the States, complaining that the *Anglo* officers did not respect him or treat him fairly. Though Concepción was currently rather annoyed at her cousin, she didn't want to dwell on the differences between his war experience and Hyde's. She was, however, keen to defend Hyde's character.

'That war-time experience is good for taking the silver to El Paso,' Concepción went on. 'Hyde knows how to travel fast across country and to stay out of sight. He only takes two other armed men with him, and the silver is carried by mule so they can travel where a wagon cannot.' She saw that Ramon was listening with interest, and expanded on Hyde's planning abilities. There had been some discussion of the next silver delivery during her visit to the mine. Concepción had picked up a good idea of the route, and Hyde had mentioned a couple of places where he thought any attack would most likely happen. She told Ramon about them, repeating what she'd been told about why those spots were risky. Her cousin listened thoughtfully, nodding to himself.

'He is thinking like a soldier,' Ramon commented when she finished talking. 'It would be difficult for anyone to take that silver against his will.'

Concepción smiled, pleased that she had impressed her cousin with Hyde's abilities. She picked out the opening of a cheerful melody on the guitar as she spoke. 'Five days from now, there will be more silver in the bank at El Paso,' she said confidently.

★ ★ ★

Ramon was grateful for the shade given by the juniper scrub. It made the long wait more endurable. Lorenzo Vargas, crouching beside him, shifted his weight and sighed loudly.

'There's more cover in the valley over that rise,' Vargas said, tilting his head to indicate the direction he meant. 'I still say we should have the ambush there.'

'It is a good place for an ambush,' Ramon agreed, keeping his voice low. 'And as I said, Hyde is a soldier, and that is the kind of place where he will be expecting an ambush. When they pass through that valley without being attacked, he will relax. He won't be expecting us here.'

Pride coloured Ramon's voice as he spoke. This planned attack was a challenge, a chance to test himself against an *Anglo* soldier. It was men like Hyde who had denied him the opportunity to show what he could do during the war. Now he was pitting his wits against Captain Hyde, and he was sure of success.

This stretch of trail certainly didn't look like a very promising place for an ambush. The best cover came from juniper and creosote brush, and from the large rocks that littered the ground. The *banditos* whom Vargas had hired had scattered themselves around, either side of the faint trail. A couple of them were hidden in depressions in the ground, with little more than some scrub or clumps of wiry grass for shade. 'The men must remember, they are not to shoot Hyde,' Ramon muttered, turning his head towards a movement just below the rise.

'I told them,' Vargas answered, yawning widely without bothering to cover his mouth.

Ramon felt a sharp stab of excitement as the scout stationed by the rise signalled to the waiting men. He pulled the dark blue bandanna up to cover his nose and mouth. Beside him, Vargas was doing the same. The indolence had gone and Vargas's eyes were bright with a subtle malice that always made Ramon uneasy. The scout had backed away now, and was hidden. Ramon could hear the soft sounds of hoofs approaching, and the occasional creak of leather. His eyes were fixed on the trail where it came over the rise, and on the rider now coming into view.

Ramon was unaware that he was smiling beneath his mask as he recognized Hyde, riding a liver chestnut horse. Hyde carried a Winchester across his lap, and scanned his surroundings as the horse walked on. A short distance behind him appeared another armed *Anglo*, then a Mexican youth leading three laden mules. The last to appear was another Mexican, also armed with a Winchester. They rode at a steady walk, heading straight into the ambush that Ramon had planned for them.

In spite of the dusty heat Hyde was still alert, his head turning from side to side as he scanned his surroundings. Ramon didn't know what had caught the Southerner's eyes, but Hyde suddenly halted his horse and began to raise his rifle. Behind him, the other men halted their mounts and came alert. The nearest bandits broke cover, bringing their own guns into line.

Hyde reacted immediately and without hesitation. His rifle spat lead at the first men to show themselves. One of the bandits spun around sharply and crashed-landed back into the creosote scrub he'd been hiding in. The man nearest to him halted his rush and dropped to one knee. More men were firing now, the crackle of rifle fire almost drowning the orders Hyde yelled to his men. He was covering their retreat, laying down fire as the two Mexicans tried to get the panicking mules to move back over the rise.

Ramon raced forward, mentally cursing Hyde for making a target of himself.

The other *Anglo* was a horse's length behind Hyde, firing at the bandits to his left, while Hyde directed his fire to the right. Clearly, Hyde had planned how to react to an ambush, but he and his men were badly outnumbered. The uneven fight couldn't last long. As the milling, frightened animals stirred up dust, Ramon saw the *Anglo* guard cry in pain and lurch sideways in his saddle, almost dropping his Winchester. The man's horse squealed as a bullet grazed its rump, and it began bucking. The injured man fell from his saddle, landing heavily, almost under the hoofs of Hyde's mount. His horse turned on its hocks and bolted back the way it had come.

A second bandit had fallen to Hyde's rifle fire, but the men remembered their orders and concentrated on the others who escorted the silver. Ramon halted, just to one side of the trail, and took a few moments to align his rifle before firing. He intended his shot to come close to Hyde's head, to remind him of his danger and to make it less obvious that he wasn't being targeted. Ramon had the satisfaction of seeing Hyde flinch momentarily, then Hyde began to swing his rifle around, seeking the new threat.

'Surrender!' Ramon shouted, keeping his rifle aligned on Hyde.

Hyde couldn't bring his rifle to bear on Ramon before the Mexican could shoot. Behind him, the mules were milling in a cloud of dust and resisting the best efforts of his men to move them. The other *Anglo* was injured and horseless. Ramon could clearly see the play of emotions on Hyde's face as the Southerner rapidly assessed his options. There was really only one choice, and Ramon had pinned Hyde to it. Hyde spread his arms out wide, holding his Winchester in his left hand.

'Stop firing,' he called.

5

Ramon barked the order to stop firing in Spanish. The last echoes of the gunshots died away as Ramon walked slowly towards Hyde, his rifle still aimed squarely at the other man.

'Drop the rifle, carefully,' Ramon ordered. He saw a grim, bitter anger in Hyde's grey eyes and recognized it as the anger of helpless frustration. To see a man like Hyde feel that frustration gave Ramon a heady feeling of power. He controlled himself though, and watched carefully as Hyde leaned to one side and let his rifle drop to the ground. 'We only want the silver,' Ramon said. Already, his men were moving towards the mules. 'All of you hand over your guns. We will empty them and leave them a short distance away.'

Vargas bent and picked up Hyde's

rifle, admiring the octagonal-barrelled Winchester.

'What about that one?' he said in Spanish, gesturing with the rifle at the wounded *Anglo*. 'I should like to see if this gun is as good as it looks.'

Ramon shook his head sharply, and replied in Spanish, 'A wounded man will slow them down; they won't follow us if they have to take care of him. Shoot the *Anglo* and they will pursue us the more.'

Vargas grunted, unsatisfied, and began extracting shells from the Winchester.

Ramon switched back to English, and told Hyde to remove his gunbelt. Pride and excitement swelled within him as Hyde obeyed his order, leaning from his saddle to drop the gunbelt to the ground.

The bandits gathered the weapons belonging to Hyde's companions and took control of the silver-laden mules. Just as Ramon had planned, his main group retreated with the mules, two of the bandit group hanging back as rearguard, to keep an eye on the defeated group from the silver mine. When the rearguard caught up, they reported that Hyde had made no attempt to follow them, and had been tending to the injured man.

'Those *Anglos* have no stomach for a fight,' Vargas said contemptuously. He hefted the Winchester and smiled. 'Hyde does not deserve such a gun.'

'We will leave the guns further along the trail as we promised,' Ramon insisted. Vargas was a dangerous man to cross, but the success of the ambush gave Ramon confidence. 'We are gentlemen and we will keep our word. And if they know we keep our word, it will be easier for them to surrender to us next time.'

A dark gleam lit Vargas's deep-set eyes. 'Next time,' he repeated with satisfaction. 'Next time.'

★ ★ ★

It was dusk by the time Hyde returned to the silver mine. Only Balzar rode with him, the young Mexican sniffing now and again as he thought of the mules taken by the bandits, along with their load. The thud of the horses' hoofs on the packed earth brought Williams out from the adobe, shotgun in his hands as he peered into the gloom in the canyon.

'Pat. It's me and Balzar,' Hyde called, his voice as dull as he felt.

'Hyde?' Williams lowered the shotgun and trotted forward to meet them. 'What's happened?' His round blue eyes were full of worry. 'Are you all right?'

Hyde reined in Cob. He felt sick inside, angry with himself. Taking a deep breath, he broke the news. 'Bandits ambushed us and took the silver. Zeke done took a bullet in the leg. He's in Hueco with Esteban; I wired for a doctor to come and see him.' He ran out of words and stopped.

Williams seemed to struggle with what he'd been told. 'An ambush?'

Hyde kicked his feet from the stirrups and dismounted, graceful in

71

spite of mental and physical weariness. 'A good one. I shot a couple of them, but they had too many guns on us, and Zeke went down quick. I had to surrender.' The last word was bitter in his mouth.

Williams put his hand on his friend's arm. 'You did right,' he said warmly. 'We can dig more silver but we can't bring anyone back to life if bandits shoot them.'

Hyde moved to let Balzar take his horse's reins. 'Three mule-loads of silver, those coyotes got,' he said sourly. Suddenly he didn't want to talk about it any more. He looked Williams straight in the eyes. 'I'm sorry,' he said brusquely, and strode away. Williams let him go, moving to speak to Balzar.

Hyde entered the adobe, blinking in the yellow light of the oil lamps, and crossed the office space to his room at the back. The room was almost dark but he didn't bother with a light. Unstrapping his gunbelt, Hyde hung it from its peg on the wall, adding his black hat. All guns had been left a little further along the trail, as the bandits had promised. The only consolation in that for Hyde was that he would have his familiar guns with him if he ever saw those bandits again. Prising off his long boots, he lay back on his bed, thinking about the bandit leader.

The bandit's clothes had been nothing out of the ordinary but, from his voice and his demeanour, Hyde guessed that he was well-born, most likely educated. That he'd kept his word and returned the guns suggested one who prided himself on being a gentleman. He'd laid the ambush well too, the thought of which made Hyde frown. Those bandits had somehow known when and where the silver was being transported. Someone at the mine must be in collaboration with the bandits. It was a problem he'd have to tackle, but not right now. Hyde sighed, stretched, and let himself relax into the straw-filled mattress. Closing his eyes, he let his thoughts drift. As happened often now, it was very soon Queenie who occupied his thoughts.

★   ★   ★

While in Hueco with the injured man, Hyde had sent a telegram to the sheriff in El Paso, as well as to a doctor. Sheriff Hill arrived at the Two Moccasin mine around noon the next day. Williams shook his hand as Balzar led the sheriff's horse to a corral.

'Thanks for coming out here,' he said.

Sheriff Hill was a little taller than Williams, and some heavier around his chest and belly. Straw-blond hair showed from under his faded, once-black hat, and his eyes were blue in a face permanently reddened by the Texas sun.

'I wanted to hear more about this here robbery,' the sheriff drawled, following as Williams led him to the office building.

Hyde was already inside, sitting behind the desk. Williams noticed that he was fiddling with his fancy pen, twisting it around between his long fingers. Hyde greeted the sheriff briefly and unsmilingly. Williams and Sheriff Hill seated themselves on the opposite side of the desk, the sheriff taking his hat off and putting it on the corner of the desk. He dug a notebook from a pocket of his baggy jacket, and flipped through it to an empty page before retrieving a stumpy pencil that looked absurdly small in his large hand.

'How much silver was taken?' he asked eventually.

Williams looked across at Hyde, who was studying the twirling pen, and answered: 'About two thousand dollars in bullion. It was being transported on three mules; two brown and one light grey.'

'Brands?'

'One brown and the grey from the Casa de las Flores; the other brown was from the J H Connected. We've got the bill of sale for all three.'

'How many men in the ambush?' Hill asked.

Hyde looked up. ' 'Bout eight or nine.'

Williams inclined his head in Hyde's direction. 'They were outnumbered more than two to one, and Hyde still brought a couple down.'

Hyde didn't look pleased at the comment, his eyebrows drawn down.

'Would you recognize any of them if you saw them again?' Hill asked.

'I reckon as I'd know the leader,' Hyde replied, his voice hard. 'He had a bandanna over his face but he wasn't a common *bandito*. He was like someone from Don Pedro's family.'

The sheriff shook his head slowly. 'I don't know of any *criollos* riding the outlaw trail.'

'Well, this one was,' Hyde insisted. He went on to give a few, brief descriptions, which Hill dutifully noted down.

'Where did they jump you?' Hill asked.

Hyde was silent for a few moments before answering. 'It was the far side of Santa Maria creek. Not in the valley, they were waiting for us over the rise.'

He fell silent again.

The sheriff grunted and turned to Williams. 'Do you-all use that route regular for transporting your silver? Travel the same day each month?'

'That's the route we mostly use,' Williams admitted. He glanced across at Hyde but the other man was staring at a spot on the wall. 'We usually ship the silver in the third week of the month,' Williams continued. 'But not the same day of the week.'

Hyde's awkward, sullen behaviour puzzled him, but he kept on talking to the sheriff. 'I spoke to every man here this morning. They all swear blind that they didn't tell anyone about the silver leaving, and I'm inclined to believe them. Half of them haven't left the canyon since we decided on the day the silver was going out anyhow.'

'Someone must have known,' Hill said. 'That ambush weren't no coincidence, sure as God made little green apples. They knew you was coming that way, and when.'

The sheriff rose, putting away the pocketbook and pencil, and donned his hat. 'I'll pass on the descriptions of the bandits. That amount of silver bullion ain't gonna be the easiest thing for them to dispose of. We may catch up with them when they try to shift it.'

Williams stood up too. 'Thank you for your help, Sheriff, we surely appreciate it.'

Hyde nodded. 'Thanks for coming out.'

Williams led the sheriff to the door. 'Come to the cookshack and have a coffee and some food before you go back. We got plenty to spare.'

'Why thank you.'

Just before following the sheriff through the door, Williams turned to look back. Hyde was still behind the desk, watching the pen as it twirled between his fingers. Williams closed the door after himself, and turned his attention to the sheriff.

★　★　★

It was suppertime when Pat Williams saw Hyde again. The tall Southerner was the last to arrive in the bunkhouse dining room. He collected a plate of stew and dumplings, and sat down opposite his partner. Williams studied him thoughtfully as they both ate. The robbery and the loss of the silver had been on his mind all day and it wasn't hard to guess that Hyde had been thinking the same way too. However, much as he wanted to, Williams decided against raising the subject again. The topic made Hyde tense and defensive, though Williams couldn't understand why. He'd said clearly that his partner had done the right thing in surrendering rather than fighting on against impossible odds. Williams cast around for another topic.

'I visited Ma and the girls yesterday afternoon,' he said. 'The whole house smelled of baked goods. They're sure cooking up a storm for the picnic.'

Hyde looked up, showing interest in something for the first time since the ambush. 'That's what, two days from now?' he asked.

Williams nodded. 'I've got a place all picked out, in Double Eagle canyon. There's some good shade, a nice clearing for the picnic and the creek widens out into a pool there.'

'Sounds plumb good,' Hyde said, and Williams was pleased to see him smile.

'Should be a real mix of foods,' Williams said. 'Ma's bringing fried chicken and pies and cake, and Conchita will be bringing Spanish food and wine.'

'It'll make a swell change from stew,' Hyde answered, stirring the brown contents of his plate. 'This ain't bad, but it'll be nice to have something that ain't stew with beans, stew with rice, stew with potatoes, or stew with dumplings.'

Williams laughed, pleased that Hyde seemed to have recovered his sense of humour.

'It'll be a good day,' he promised.

6

It was a colourful, cheerful party that rode into Double Eagle canyon. Williams led the way, with Conchita riding beside him. She was as bright as a flower in her elaborate green and gold dress, the many ruffles on the skirt fluttering in the light breeze. Behind them came Mrs Williams, driving a buggy, with Caitlin beside her. Queenie rode alongside the buggy, sitting sidesaddle on a well bred grey horse. Hyde was riding at the back of the main group, along with Don Pedro; he took the opportunity to study Queenie discreetly. She wore a dusky green dress that set off her glowing red hair to perfection. The neatly braided and coiled hair was partly concealed under a broad-brimmed oatstraw hat that shaded her porcelain complexion from the Texas sun. Not only was she beautiful, but Hyde noted how well she rode the grey mare, her gloved hands light on the reins.

Double Eagle canyon was beautiful, lush with trees and grass. Half a dozen pronghorns erupted from the long grass and bounded away, soon lost to sight. Williams led the party to a clearing by the creek, where cottonwoods and hackberry trees provided shade, and wild roses scented the air. The group dismounted and allowed the horses to drink from the creek before tethering them to picket ropes in the shade. One of the servants from the hacienda had accompanied them, leading a mule laden with Don Pedro's contribution to the picnic. The servant spread colourful rugs on the grass, and began serving to the hungry group.

Hyde felt himself relaxing as the excellent food was eaten, and rich red wine drunk. The humiliation of being ambushed and forced to surrender his guns and silver had been festering inside him. He knew he'd been abrupt with Williams every time the topic had come up, but he found it very hard to talk about his failure, and the way he'd let his partner down. Now that a few days had passed, the feelings were less acute and easier to cope with.

Besides, life didn't seem so bad in good company like this. The women, in their beautiful dresses, the good food and general air of leisure, reminded him of his comfortable life among the wealthy of South Carolina, before the Civil War. A year back, the thought of all that he had lost in the war, including the deaths of his father and younger brother, as well as the loss of the family's money and estates, would have filled him with a sullen anger. Now the days of desperation and poverty were behind him. He could afford to support his mother and widowed sister, who still lived back in Charleston. His life held promise once more, with friends like Pat Williams.

And for the first time in years, Hyde found himself thinking about the future, rather than simply getting by in the present. He looked over at Queenie, who was with her horse, and marvelled at the sudden impact she'd had on his feelings. And, most wonderfully, she seemed to like him in return. Not with the calculated interest of her sister, Caitlin, who was too obviously looking for 'a good catch'. There was an honesty about Queenie that fascinated him as much as her striking beauty.

Hyde got up, and strolled over to join her by the horses. She looked round as he approached, and greeted him with a smile that warmed him through.

'Are you enjoying yourself?' she asked.

'I sure am,' Hyde replied, smiling at her in return.

The grey horse had lifted its head as he approached. Hyde stroked its velvety muzzle, and chuckled as the grey nuzzled his jacket pocket.

'Sorry, nothing for you to eat there,' he said, pushing the horse's head away. 'This is a good horse, you've got here,' he went on. 'What's she called?'

Queenie smiled. 'She didn't have a name, so I called her Titania.'

The name sounded vaguely familiar to Hyde, who frowned as he thought about it.

'That's from Shakespeare, isn't it? Something to do with fairies?'

Queenie nodded, looking slightly self-conscious. 'Titania's the queen of the fairies in *A Midsummer Night's Dream*. It just seemed to suit her,' she added, stroking the grey horse's neck. 'Caitlin suggested calling her Cloudy.'

'Cloudy's nice, but Titania's a heap more imaginative,' Hyde said admiringly. 'I surely know more about horses than I do about Shakespeare, mind.'

'Your Cob looks like a good horse too,' Queenie said, looking over at Hyde's liver chestnut.

Hyde smiled warmly. 'He is too. He's one of the last foaled on our estate, and I rode him though the last couple of years of the war. He's as brave as a lion.'

'I like his eye,' Queenie replied. 'He looks a bold sort.'

'He sure is.'

They continued talking easily about horses, exploring their shared interest in them.

Hyde had turned himself a little so he could easily watch the rest of the picnic group. He most often glanced at Williams, but to his inner relief, his partner's attention was entirely on Conchita, whose lilting voice and giggles made a merry tune in the group's conversations. Hyde knew that sooner or later, he'd have to speak to Williams about Queenie, but the time didn't seem right just now. He knew Williams cared deeply about his family, but didn't know how he'd react to the idea of his youngest sister marrying someone fourteen years older than herself. With the worry of the ambush and robbery so close, Hyde didn't want Williams to be worrying about his sister as well.

Time spent with Queenie seemed to

fly past, but Hyde was aware that he couldn't spent too long talking alone with her. As they talked, the others spread out, with Conchita settling herself at the edge of the creek, dipping her hands in the cool water as she chatted to Williams, and splashing him playfully now and again. Don Pedro was talking to Mrs Williams and Caitlin. The girl wasn't paying much attention to de la Valle, but was studying Conchita's dress, and fluffing out the ruffles on her own.

Reluctantly, Hyde said, 'It's not proper for me to keep your attention to myself. We'd best go join the others.'

Queenie glanced across at the other picnickers. 'I reckon you're right,' she said without much enthusiasm. However, as they started to walk, she smiled at Hyde in a way that made him feel warm inside. He led her back across the clearing to the rest of the group.

They were about halfway back when there was a sharp squeal from behind. Hyde spun round and saw the buggy horse lash out at Conchita's bay mare. The bay squealed in pain at the kick and reared back, pulling on her tether. The short post she was tied to came free from the ground and swung towards her, hitting the mare on her forelegs. Frightened, the mare screamed and plunged forward into a gallop, bolting blindly in the direction of the picnickers sitting on the grass. The post swung back and forth as she ran, hitting her on the legs again and increasing her terror.

'Stay there!' Hyde snapped at Queenie.

He ran to intercept the bolting mare. Williams was scrambling to his feet over by the creek, but he couldn't reach the horse before it charged through the space where Don Pedro, his mother and sister were. Don Pedro and Mrs Williams were also starting to move, but Caitlin just screamed, frozen in panic. Hyde sprinted across the grass, running to meet the terrified horse at an angle. Don Pedro had made his feet and was offering a hand to Mrs

Williams, who was the closest to him. She staggered as she trod on her long skirt and the heavy man took her weight. The bay mare was heading directly towards them, but was galloping in blind fear, the whites of her eyes showing.

Hyde ran flat out, mentally cursing each time the tethering post banged against the mare's legs and frightened her more. Conchita was on her feet, calling her mare's name in calming tones, but Caitlin's screams almost drowned her out. Hyde saw that he wasn't going to reach the mare's head before she passed him. Throwing himself desperately forward, he got one hand on the trailing rope.

'Whooooaa!'

He was almost dragged off his feet by the bolting horse, but managed to maintain his balance. The bouncing post smacked him hard in the leg but he hardly noticed. Hyde got hold of the rope with both hands and leaned his weight back, digging the heels of his boots into the ground. The mare's head turned towards him, though she was still moving, dragging him after her step by step.

'Whoa. Whoa there, girl,' Hyde repeated in low, calming tones, as the mare plunged at the end of the rope. The mare snorted and kicked out, but she was no longer moving forwards. Controlling his gasps for breath, Hyde continued the soothing noises as he changed his grip, getting closer to the mare's head. She reared and struck at him with a foreleg, but Hyde was out of her reach. He let the rope slide through his hands as she reared and tightened his grip again as soon as she came down. The post was no longer banging against her legs, and her ears pricked forward in response to Hyde's continued soothing.

Conchita approached at a brisk walk, knowing better than to run towards a nervous horse, adding her familiar voice and Spanish endearments to Hyde's tones. As she passed Hyde, she spoke to him, looking at her horse and speaking in the same tone of voice. '*Gracias, señor, gracias.*'

The mare, trembling with fright, stretched out her nose towards her mistress. Conchita patted the horse on the neck and began calming her.

Satisfied that Conchita could control the horse, though still keeping hold of the rope, Hyde looked around at the others. Caitlin was on her feet now, sobbing in her mother's arms and complaining of her fright. Pat Williams was standing nearby, patting his sister on the shoulder. He caught Hyde's gaze, sending him a look of relief and gratitude. Hyde smiled in return, glancing across at Queenie, who was moving to join her mother and sister. Don Pedro was approaching, moving with surprising grace for such a bulky man. He was praising Hyde for his quick thinking and courage.

Hyde gave him the mare's rope and walked over to join Williams. Although his actions had been purely instinctive, he felt he had at least partly redeemed himself for his failure to protect the silver. He had protected Williams's family, more precious by far than any silver. Williams came to meet him, clapping him on the shoulder as his good-natured face widened into a smile.

'Looks like I owe you another favour,' he said.

'You'd have done the same iffen you'd been in the right place,' Hyde replied.

'I'd have tried, for certain-sure,' Williams agreed. 'But there's no guarantee I'd have caught that rope.'

'I'm just glad I did,' Hyde said honestly.

Williams smiled again. 'The whole family's plumb glad you did. A man couldn't ask for a better friend than you.'

Hyde glanced at Queenie, and smiled too.

★ ★ ★

Ramon Morales paused in the doorway of the cantina, sniffing fastidiously at the smells coming from within. Hueco was a small town, but it had at least one cantina that was better quality than this one. However, this was where he had agreed to meet Lorenzo Vargas, so Ramon swallowed his disgust at the stale smells, straightened himself to look as tall as possible, and went in. Inside, the adobe cantina was cool and dim. Ramon suspected that the dim light had the advantage that it made it harder for patrons to see just how dirty the place was. Not that the *peon* he walked past seemed overly concerned by dirt, judging by the food stains on his once-white shirt.

Vargas was at a table close to the entertainment, which was a pretty, albeit rabbit-toothed girl, plucking a guitar. Ramon swiped his white handkerchief across a chair before sitting down. Vargas looked at him, his deep-set eyes mocking.

'I guess you heard about Señor Hyde

making himself a hero by catching a horse?' he said.

Ramon answered in Spanish. 'The horse would have jumped over anyone on the ground. They very rarely trample anyone.'

Vargas answered in the same language. 'This one was in a blind panic. Horses in that state will run over cliffs.'

Ramon knew this was true, but didn't feel inclined to give Hyde credit for his actions. 'I could have done the same if I'd been there,' he insisted. 'I had more important business to take care of.'

He stopped speaking to give his order to the serving girl who had approached the table. She smiled and simpered, her eyes calculating the cost of his good clothes. Vargas smiled, and gave her a hearty slap on the behind as she passed him.

'Not good enough for your tastes,' he told Ramon. 'But a girl like that knows how to keep a man warm in bed.'

Ramon grunted by way of answer,

disgust evident in his eyes. Vargas just laughed.

'Tell me then, how did your business go in El Paso?'

Ramon allowed himself a smile. '*Bueno*. I sold the packmules without any trouble, and took a bar of the silver over the border. I have plenty of money now to pay for more men.'

Vargas grinned, his eyes lighting up. 'So when do we get to take more silver from the damn *Anglos?*'

'I think it will be two or three more weeks.' Ramon broke off as the girl returned and served his beer.

As she started to move away, Vargas grabbed her and pulled her into his lap, kissing her while feeling her breasts. She struggled, swatting at the hand groping her. Vargas finished his kiss and released her. The flustered girl got to her feet, cursing him and glaring. Vargas chuckled and dug a silver coin from his pocket to toss at her. The serving girl spat at him, swooping down to pick up the coin, and stamped off. Vargas grinned.

'With a temper like that, she'd be a hot one in bed!'

Ramon hid his reaction to his cousin's actions; a serving girl hardly deserved the same degree of respect as a lady like Concepción, but a gentleman treated all women with a degree of honour. He took a long drink of the beer before speaking.

'I'll keep talking to Conchita,' Ramon said, returning to the topic of the mine. 'She's always keen to talk about how clever Williams and Hyde are. She'll tell me about the next delivery of bullion if I ask her right.'

Vargas chuckled. 'She's a pretty little thing but no smarter than any other woman. So long as she does what men tell her to do, that's all that matters. That and providing her husband with sons.'

Ramon nodded agreement, though he wouldn't have put things so crudely himself. Still, he reminded himself, Vargas did have his uses.

'I want you to get the same men again, as far as you can,' he said. 'The fewer who know of our involvement, the better.'

Vargas grinned in anticipation. 'I wonder if they'll put up a better fight than they did last time. Those cowardly *Anglos* surrendered very quickly.'

'My ambush gave them no choice,' Ramon said proudly. 'Hyde was a soldier, he's smart enough to know when to surrender and save lives.'

Vargas tossed back the remains of his tequila with a sharp movement. 'He's a coward. And why do you talk of him with respect? An *Anglo* knows nothing of honour and doesn't deserve it from us.'

'Hyde may be an *Anglo*, but he is still a gentleman,' Ramon insisted, knowing that his cousin wouldn't believe him. 'But Conchita and the Casa de las Flores are too precious to fall into the hands of an *Anglo*, especially a common one like that Williams. I shall get rid of Williams, and

Hyde too, because of his loyalty to Williams. This I swear, on the blood of my ancestors.'

Vargas grinned, challenge in his eyes as he looked at Ramon. 'You talk like a man. I look forward to seeing you act like one.'

Ramon stared straight back at him. 'You will.'

7

Pat Williams stepped outside the smelting plant, and took a deep breath of the fresh air. This canyon was no longer as pretty as the one where they'd had their eventful picnic a few days ago, but the lumber buildings, corrals and even the pile of tailings filled him with a sense of pride. This valley was a thriving silver mine, and his name was one of the two on the deeds. As he looked at his domain, Williams saw his partner, Hyde emerge from the office, carrying his saddle, and head for the nearby small corral.

Williams went to meet him, crossing the creek by the stepping stones they'd laid during the winter. Balzar was already at the corral, and took Hyde's tack, eager to handle the horse himself. Hyde handed over the range saddle and bridle with a resigned air, and lounged against the corral rails. Williams smiled as he approached.

'That boy sure loves your horse,' he remarked, looking at Balzar as the young man carefully settled the saddle on the chestnut's back.

'Sure, an' he looks after them all real swell,' Hyde replied. 'But he surely does love Cob. I'm surprised he lets me ride him.'

Williams chuckled. 'Where are you going?'

'Mostly I'm just aiming to give Cob some exercise. I might take a look at alternative routes for taking the silver to El Paso,' Hyde replied off-handedly.

Williams glanced at his own horse, drowsing in the corral. 'Maybe I'll join you.'

'There's no need,' Hyde protested. When Williams looked at him, Hyde went on. 'Well, I guess perhaps I just want to get out on my own for a while.'

'Ah.' Williams smiled to show he wasn't offended. He was used to Hyde's occasional need for solitude, and his desire to get away from the noise of the mine. 'I'll not bother you then.'

Hyde showed his sharklike smile. 'I surely appreciate that, *amigo*.'

He turned to Balzar, who had led his horse to the gate of the corral. Hyde did a quick, automatic check of his horse's tack, and thanked the wrangler. Mounting gracefully, he nodded to Williams and rode away at a brisk walk.

'Are you going to ride?' Balzar asked in Spanish.

'Not now,' Williams replied. 'I reckon I'll go out in the evening though.'

He watched Hyde riding away down the canyon before returning to the smelting plant, refreshed by his brief break from the noise and smell.

* * *

Hyde walked his horse for the first few minutes, letting Cob warm up, then consulted a gold pocket-watch. Putting the watch back, he pushed his horse

101

into a jog, his face eager as they left the hills behind and headed towards Hueco. It seemed to take far longer than usual to get close to the little town. At last, as he topped a rise, Hyde picked out another mounted figure waiting just below another ridge to the east of town. He nudged his horse into a lope, feasting his eyes on the sight of Queenie Williams, waiting on her grey mare.

She smiled as he pulled up beside her, deftly controlling the grey as it side-stepped away from Cob. Hyde swept off his hat and bowed.

'I sure hope I'm not late,' he drawled.

'I don't think so,' Queenie answered. 'I've only been here a few minutes, and I've been enjoying the scenery and watching the birds.'

'Good,' Hyde replied. 'Which way would you like to ride?'

'I still hardly know the country around here,' Queenie answered. 'You choose someplace.'

Hyde nodded, and turned his horse

southwards. Queenie moved her grey alongside him; the two horses snorted companionably at one another.

'When are you expected back?' Hyde asked.

'Not till suppertime,' she told him. 'I told Ma I was going to look for eagles, and other interesting birds.'

'You're interested in wild animals then?'

'Yes. Mostly I just love being outdoors, and riding, and seeing the country. And this is new country.'

'Have you travelled much?' Hyde asked.

Queenie shook her head, the wild-flowers on the brim of her neat straw hat bobbing with the movement. 'Central Texas is all I know, though it feels like I know Ireland, after hearing Momma and Poppa talk about it so much. You must have travelled some, though?'

'I've seen some of the South,' Hyde said. 'Before the War, we used to travel about, visiting kin and staying for a few weeks. Afterwards I drifted down to

Texas, and saw the plains for the first time.'

Queenie smiled. 'I bet this country's a heap different from South Carolina.'

'It sure is,' Hyde replied emphatically. He glanced about at the landscape they were riding through. It was dry, shrubby country, dotted with creosote bush, agave, clumps of grasses and the thin branches of Mormon Tea. Here and there, the long whips of the ocotillo cactus, tipped with red flowers, waved in the breeze. Other plants were in bloom too, brightening the faded earth tones of the desert. In spite of the flowers though, the land still looked bleak compared to the lush, green country where he'd grown up.

'I'd sure admire to see the Rockies,' Queenie told him, turning her face westwards.

'If I hadn't settled here with Pat, I'd have headed over that way,' Hyde said. 'Cousin Boyd visited Colorado before the war, and it sounds like beautiful country there.'

'Oh, yes,' Queenie agreed. 'I've seen pictures but they weren't good enough. I'd love to see it for myself.'

Hyde caught himself on the point of saying that they would go to Colorado for their honeymoon. The realization of what he'd been about to say startled him. He'd only known Queenie Williams for a matter of weeks, and they'd spent less than a full day in one another's company. Yet he felt comfortable in her company, and every time he looked at her, at the vivid red hair, white skin and slanting green eyes, he was struck anew with how lovely she was. Now, he looked at her a little uncertainly. He was thirteen years older than she, and a woman so beautiful surely had other suitors to choose from.

Queenie smiled at him, and Hyde found himself smiling back and relaxing. After all, it was his company she'd chosen today; no one else's.

'I hear that New England is beautiful in the fall, when the trees change colour,' he said.

'Oh yes, I'd like to see that too. And if I ever have the money, I'd visit old England — London.'

They rode together, chatting about places they'd like to see, and places they had been. Hyde discovered that Queenie had the same gift for telling amusing tales as her brother. With their absorbing interest in one another, the time flew by. Queenie was the first to notice the sun's position in the sky.

'My hat!' she exclaimed, looking around. 'How far are we from town? I should be getting back.'

Hyde glanced about, getting his bearings as he mentally cursed himself for not paying attention. 'We should be back by dusk if we trot most of the way,' he told her. 'The horses haven't done much work really, so we can hustle some.'

They turned and set off for Hueco at a brisk jog. Both horses pricked their ears and strode out eagerly, knowing they were returning home. They had covered roughly half the distance back when Queenie's grey suddenly stumbled, throwing her rider forward. Queenie kept her balance and helped the horse stay on its feet. Hyde noticed her clever riding even as he stopped and turned his own horse.

'I think she may have stepped in a hole,' Queenie said, peering down at her horse's legs.

Hyde nodded. 'Walk her on, would you?'

Queenie obeyed, but it was quickly clear to both of them that the mare was lame on her off fore. Hyde dismounted, and handed Cob's reins to Queenie. He put a hand on the horse's shoulder, noting her reaction, and slowly moved his hand down the leg, examining it carefully. When he lifted the mare's hoof, the problem was apparent.

'This shoe's almost off,' Hyde said, cradling the raised hoof with both hands. 'I reckon she overreached herself and wrenched the shoe.'

Overreaching happened when a horse caught the back of a front foot with one of the hind feet. The grey had trodden on her own heel, trapping the shoe, and had partly ripped the shoe away when she'd tried to move the trapped foot.

He heard a soft sound that might have been a curse from Queenie before she spoke aloud. 'Can you remove it? Titania can't walk properly with it twisted like that.'

Hyde tugged at the shoe, but it was still sturdily fastened around the toe of the hoof. With no tools, he had no chance of removing it, and told Queenie so.

'Best I can do is try to hammer it as flat as I can, so she can walk on it, but she won't be able to carry weight. You won't be able to ride her.'

'You'd better help me down then.'

Releasing the hoof, Hyde moved around in front of the patient mare. Queenie released her left foot from the single stirrup, and swung her legs clear of the sidesaddle's pommels. Sitting sideways on the grey's back, she held out her left hand. Hyde took her hand to support her as she sprang lightly down to the ground. She left her hand in his, as she adjusted the skirt of her habit, and when she eventually removed it and smiled at him, he could still feel the warmth of her touch against his skin.

'I should ask Ma again about riding cross-saddle,' Queenie remarked. 'It would make mounting and dismounting so much easier, especially if I'm out on my own.'

'Sidesaddle's more elegant,' Hyde replied. 'But I reckon cross-saddle is more practical out West.'

Queenie held the mare's reins, speaking soothingly to her, as Hyde used the butt of one of his matched guns to hammer the shoe more or less flat. Queenie led her horse forward, and after a couple of cautious steps, the grey mare moved evenly. Queenie patted her mare's neck, and smiled at Hyde.

'That's swell, thank you. Titania may have a sore foot by the time we get home, but at least we'll get home.'

'We'd best be getting on,' Hyde reminded her. 'It's surely going to be past suppertime by the time you get home.'

In spite of Queenie's protests, Hyde switched saddles, and then legged her up so she was riding Cob.

'I walk faster than you,' he said firmly. 'We'll get back to Hueco quicker iffen you ride and I walk.'

Hyde's long legs and wiry strength enabled them to keep up a good pace, but the sun was setting behind them. After an hour's steady walk, dusk was in the air, and it wouldn't be long before full dark. Queenie reined in Cob, and looked down.

'Titania isn't lame. If we kept to soft ground, I think she could manage some spells of trotting.'

Hyde's boots were better designed for riding than for walking and his feet were already sore. He patted the mare's neck as he spoke.

'I don't know as I could jog far enough to make a difference,' he admitted. 'We'd only be jogging very short spells.'

'Switch the saddles back, and I'll ride behind you,' Queenie said. 'I'm sure Cob can carry us double, as we're not going faster than a trot.'

The suggestion made sense, but Hyde still hesitated. He'd been raised with the traditional, strict manners of the old South. Riding double with a young lady simply wasn't done, and the lady's reputation would be ruined. Times had changed though, and common sense told him that it was more important to get Queenie back to town before dark. As well as the natural dangers like pumas and aggressive steers, there was also the chance of encountering bandits and wandering Comanche bucks. The need to protect Queenie from physical danger won out over the values of a past way of life.

Hyde began unfastening the girth of the saddle on the mare. 'My mammy would be shocked to her soul, but making tracks for home's more important.'

In a few minutes, the saddles had been transferred back to their original mounts. Hyde shortened his stirrups, legged Queenie up into his saddle, and waited while she did her best to arrange the skirt of her habit so it covered her while sitting astride the saddle. When she was done, he lashed the grey's reins to his saddle, and vaulted up behind Queenie. Cob's ears flickered back and forth at the unusual experience, but Queenie spoke quietly to him and he stayed calm.

'Are you comfortable?' she asked.

The saddle skirt was nothing like as comfortable as the seat, but Hyde was more uncomfortable about sitting right behind Queenie. The plaited coil of her red hair was a few inches from his face; his hands brushed against the fabric of her skirt and she was all but in his lap.

'I'm fine,' he said rather succinctly, and pressed his heels into Cob's sides to get the horse moving.

Queenie laughed as Cob broke into a trot.

'I guess I'm getting some practice at riding cross-saddle after all.'

Cob's trot was very smooth, but the motion was enough to bump them gently together from time to time. Hyde was a good rider, but perched on the saddle skirt, and without his stirrups, he sometimes had to balance himself by holding on to Queenie for a few moments. He apologized each time, but Queenie wasn't upset.

'Just imagine that we're dancing,' she said. 'You'd be holding me if we were waltzing, and this is no different.'

With that reassurance, Hyde relaxed a little, and used her to steady himself when necessary. All the same, being so close to her was a bitter-sweet pleasure. Hyde longed to wrap his arms around her, and to kiss her neck. Queenie never flinched when he touched her, but she kept her gaze forward so he was unable to read what was in her clear green eyes. She began telling him some anecdotes about her sisters and he concentrated on what she was saying, harmlessly occupying his mind. As they rode on, he became more engrossed in the conversation and almost forgot their physical closeness.

Titania began to limp after a while and they had to slow to a walk. However, they'd made up enough time for them to reach the outskirts of Hueco not too long after dark. They circled the little town to reach Queenie's home, keeping away from lamplight and the people out enjoying the cooler night air. At last they were close enough for Hyde to dismount and help her down from the saddle. She took the mare's reins from him, and smiled at him in the low light.

'Thank you for your company, Robson. I had a lovely day.'

'So did I,' he replied simply. 'I'd like to ride with you again sometime.'

'I'd like that too, but we'll have to wait until Titania's sound again.'

'I don't mind waiting,' Hyde said. He tipped his hat to her. 'Good night, Miss Queenie.'

'Good night,' she answered softly. She looked at him a moment longer, then turned her horse and walked away.

Hyde watched her return safely to her home, then lengthened his stirrups and remounted. Cob set off back towards the mine at a brisk pace, his ears pricked. Hyde rubbed his knuckles on his horse's neck.

'I expect you're wanting to get home and get a good feed,' he said to the horse. Cob snorted in reply, making Hyde grin.

★ ★ ★

The Two Moccasins mine was a much more peaceful place in the evening. The thudding of the stamp mill had ceased, and the soft darkness hid almost all signs of the mine workings. Pat Williams could just make out the dark shape of the smelter on the other side of the creek but the other working buildings were lost in the night. Williams was sitting outside the office, intermittently reading a book by golden lamp light. Most of the other mine staff were clustered outside the bunkhouse, playing cards and listening to Pepe strumming his guitar. The tabby cat appeared from some scrub bushes, its eyes glowing like opals in the lantern light. A deer mouse was hanging limply from its mouth. The cat uttered a muffled chirrup, and faded back into the twilight.

The peace was disturbed by an alarm call from a quail near the mouth of the canyon. Williams lowered the book and looked that way, noticing that his horse had lifted its head and was peering over the corral fence at the path. The bay pricked its ears and gave a low whinny of welcome, which reassured Williams. A few moments later, he saw Hyde and Cob emerge from the darkness and ride up to the corral.

Putting his book down, Williams went to greet his friend.

'Pepe's kept you some supper,' he said.

Hyde dismounted, landing a little stiffly. 'Thanks, I'm pretty damn hungry.' He bent and began unfastening the saddle's cinch.

Williams stroked Cob's face. 'I reckoned you might be. I was expecting you back some time afore now,' he added conversationally.

'Yeah, I . . . went a mite further afield than I reckoned to,' Hyde drawled, lifting the heavy saddle clear of his horse's back. As he folded the girth over the seat, and put the saddle on the top rail of the corral, Balzar came up and took Cob's reins from Williams. The horse nuckered softly and pushed its muzzle towards the young man.

'Rub him down well and give him a good feed,' Hyde instructed. 'He's done a heap of work today.'

'*Sí, señor*.' Balzar slipped the bridle off and handed it to Hyde, before leading Cob into the corral with no more than a hand on the horse's neck.

Hyde placed the bridle over the seat of the saddle and picked it up, turning towards the office. Williams walked the short distance with him, expecting to hear more about his friend's ride. When no information was volunteered, he simply asked.

'I take it you had a good ride, then?'

Hyde looked at him, somewhat startled. 'Yes. Yes, I did.' He paused, emotions flickering through his grey eyes. 'Sorry I was away from the business for so long.'

'That's all right,' Williams answered truthfully. Hyde was a hard worker, and Williams knew from experience that when he went out for a ride, he would spend the evening at his desk to catch up if necessary. What puzzled him this evening was the impression he got that Hyde was somehow being evasive. Hyde wasn't a chatty man, and Williams hadn't expected to hear much about his ride, but he felt that Hyde was uncomfortable talking about it. What Hyde got up to outside the mine was his own business, of course, and so Williams let the subject drop. Maybe he would ask Conchita if she had any idea of what Hyde had been doing. Growing up with three sisters had taught him that women knew far more about these things than men.

'You put your tack away and I'll get Pepe to start heating up some supper for you,' he told Hyde cheerfully. He gave his friend an affectionate slap on the shoulder and headed for the bunkhouse.

8

'Are you sure they'll be coming this way?' Vargas asked peevishly.

Ramon stifled a sigh of irritation, and glanced sideways at his stocky cousin. They were waiting in the cover of a sprawling juniper bush, the plant's resinous smell strong in the dry air.

'This is the route Conchita told me two days ago,' he repeated. Needled by Vargas' disbelieving look, he continued: 'Hyde naturally tells his partner, Williams, his route to El Paso. Williams sees nothing wrong in telling his fiancée, Conchita.'

'And Conchita naturally tells her cousin?' Vargas growled.

'Like I told you, Conchita wants to think the best of Williams and his partner. So when I cast doubts on Hyde's skill as a soldier, she defends him by telling me how clever he is. And to show how clever, she tells me the route he has planned, and how this will avoid any *bandito* ambushes.'

Vargas snorted and shook his head. 'Conchita's a pretty thing, but she's as stupid as all other women. There's only two uses for any woman; one's in the kitchen and the other's in the bedroom. I'd like to get Conchita in my bedroom one night, preferably before she marries that Williams, so he's getting used goods . . . '

Ramon twisted, pushing his face up close to Vargas's and staring straight into his cousin's deep-set eyes.

'Never speak of her in those terms!' he hissed. 'She is Doña Concepción Maria Flores de la Valle. She is not to be spoken of like a common serving girl!'

Vargas stared back, his eyes calculating whether or not to challenge Ramon's order. Ramon usually backed down from their confrontations, but he drew on his anger to keep his gaze firm. After a few moments, Vargas shrugged casually.

'She's still just a woman,' he remarked.

'But a woman who deserves respect,' Ramon insisted. He moved back and turned away, not wanting to push his intolerant cousin any further.

They went back to waiting in silence. Ramon thought over his plan again, considering different outcomes. His first ambush had been a complete success, which had increased his confidence for this one. They were waiting a couple of hundred yards from the mouth of a wide, gently-curving arroyo. The arroyo itself had some trees and scrub cover, which made it a likely spot for an ambush. So Ramon, Vargas and half a dozen hardcases were outside the arroyo, hidden among the juniper and creosote bush. Ramon knew that Hyde wasn't stupid, and after the first ambush, would be expecting attack at less likely places. Ramon was playing a game of bluff and double-bluff, knowing that Hyde couldn't remain fully alert every mile of the way from the mine to El Paso.

Ramon was thinking of the next ambush, and wondering whether to chose a more obvious site next time, or whether Hyde would be expecting him to change his pattern, when the lookout near the arroyo signalled the approach of the silver carriers. Tugging his bandanna up over his face, he felt his heart start to pound as he levered a shell into the chamber of his rifle. Vargas had done the same, a feral gleam in his eyes as he waited impatiently.

Hyde came into view first, his rifle carried across his lap as his head turned, surveying the landscape. A few yards behind him rode a man whom Ramon vaguely recognized as one of Señor de la Valle's men; he too had a rifle in his hands. After them came three more men, each leading two packmules, and another armed *Anglo* brought up the rear. Hyde had more men that Ramon had expected, and all looked to be capable fighters this time. However, Hyde was still outnumbered, and Ramon's group had the advantage of surprise. Ramon tensed, waiting for Hyde to reach the ideal spot before he launched the ambush.

As he waited, a quail ran out from a clump of grass close to where Hyde's horse was passing. The bird scurried towards a larger clump of creosote bush, then suddenly changed direction and scooted away, uttering its alarm call. Hyde immediately straightened, the rifle swinging to align on the bush that the bird had fled from.

'Back!' he ordered, his voice clear and calm.

Ramon lunged from his hiding-place, Vargas and his men following suit. Hyde's rifle fired first, and a mercenary collapsed before he'd even got to his feet. The men with the mules were turning and retreating to the arroyo, while Hyde and Costilla, Don Pedro's man, swept the ground with rifle fire. Ramon was flushed with fury that his carefully planned ambush had been set off too soon, and all because of a stupid bird. His temper affected his aim, and his first shots went wild.

As before, the men had strict orders not to shoot Hyde. The packmules had turned by the time Ramon's men were clear of their hiding-places, and were galloping back to the shelter of the arroyo, which was much closer to them than Ramon had intended. Bullets tore through shrubs and kicked up dirt, but none made contact with the fleeing men. One of the mules brayed as it was hit. It fell and lay kicking, unable to rise again. Costilla turned and retreated at an order from Hyde, who was still firing with deadly speed and accuracy.

Three of Ramon's men were down, two unmoving and one painfully crawling back into cover. The other men were slowing their rate of fire, preferring to seek cover. Ramon saw the

Winchester turn his way and dropped to one knee. He fired back, trying to hit or scare Hyde's horse, but his shot ploughed up dry dirt a couple of feet to the chestnut's right.

There was a yell from Costilla, who had reached the mouth of the arroyo. Hyde fired a last shot, which cracked past Ramon's ear, then spun his horse and fled at a flat-out gallop. Costilla was covering Hyde's retreat, but he was further away and less accurate. As Ramon scrambled to his feet again, he saw Vargas lining his rifle on Hyde.

'No!' Ramon slashed out with his own rifle, knocking Vargas's aside and spoiling his shot. Vargas turned to glare at him and, for a moment, Ramon thought the rifle was about to be turned on him.

'We need Hyde and Williams to fight, remember?' he hissed. 'We let the *Anglos* destroy themselves.'

Vargas held his breath for a moment, then let it out in an explosive snort, as he shook his head to clear it. As he relaxed, so did Ramon, who turned to see Hyde reaching the mouth of the arroyo. He was crouched low over his horse's neck as it galloped, his head turned to look back at the ambush. A couple of shots were fired after him, but to no effect. Then he was out of sight, following the rest of the silver escort.

'We didn't hit one of them,' Vargas grumbled.

'The intention wasn't to kill,' Ramon reminded him. 'We still got some of the silver, on that mule, but that's a bonus. Hyde has to explain to Williams that he was attacked again, and that he's lost more of their silver. Now we start spreading the rumours that Hyde is involved in the robberies — that he's getting a big share of the stolen money.' Ramon paused and smiled. 'Don't you think it's strange that the bandits don't seem to shoot at him? You might almost think that he and they were on the same side.'

Vargas's face twisted into a malicious grin. 'Cousin, you are far more devious than I had believed. That is a compliment.'

The praise warmed Ramon, who stood straight and proud, looking in the direction that Hyde had gone. Anything seemed possible now.

* * *

Hyde soon caught up with the rest of his group. They headed back through the arroyo at a good pace, Hyde at the rear in case of pursuit. When they had travelled a couple of miles, Hyde called for them to halt and regroup. They gathered together, horses and mules blowing, at the end of a straight section of the arroyo, giving themselves a good lead if chasers should appear around the distant corner.

'Is anyone hurt?' Hyde asked, levering more shells into his rifle. To his relief, everyone shook their heads.

'I'm plumb sorry about losing the mule,' Busby said. 'It were one toting silver, too.'

'It wasn't your fault,' Hyde told him.

'We were lucky just to lose the one mule this time.' He looked around at each one of his men, presenting them with an outwardly controlled appearance. His horse was turned so he could half-see the curve where pursuers might appear, but he could still see all of his men.

'You did a good job in spotting the ambush,' Costillo told him. 'It was the quail, wasn't it? I didn't think anything of that, when it changed direction.'

'I learned a lot during the war,' Hyde replied, his tone closing the subject.

'If we'd been further away from the arroyo . . . '

'If we'd been right among them . . . '

Hyde ignored the conversations as the men talked, working through their excitement and experiences. He was pleased to have escaped the ambush, and that his plan had worked, but he was troubled by the fact of the ambush itself. Once again, the bandits had been in the right place at the right time. Somehow, they had got to know the time and route of his journey to El Paso. Hyde knew full well that he'd discussed his plan for this trip with no one but Pat Williams. He didn't want to believe that Pat would deliberately betray their partnership like this. Pushing the thought to one side, he set about reorganizing the trek to El Paso.

'We'll swing around to the south,' he told the others. 'The trail's dry for near on a day's ride, but we'll water the animals and refill the canteens at Screech Owl Creek. It'll be dark when we do the last few miles of the dry stretch, and cooler then.'

'What about the *banditos*?' Esteban asked.

'If they wanted to try again, they'd be after us right now,' Hyde said straight-forwardly. 'I don't reckon they'll cut across country and try to intercept us. They don't know whether we'll take the north or the south route, or if we'd turn tail and go back to the mine. They'd have to carry the silver off that mule while they try to find us, and chances are they'd be riding in the wrong direction. Whoever their leader is, he's cautious. He won't ride about, hoping to get lucky and find us again.'

The men nodded, accepting Hyde's confident assessment. After a brief check of horses and equipment, they were on their way again. Although Hyde was riding scout again, his mind kept wandering to thoughts of how the bandits were getting their information, and Williams's part in it. He'd been stunned when Pat Williams had made him a full partner in the new mine, the year before. It had been a generous gesture on Williams's part but was he regretting it now? Perhaps with the arrival of his family, and his marriage to Conchita becoming a reality, Pat was regretting his kindness.

Hyde shook his head. He couldn't reconcile that thought with the generous good nature he'd consistently seen from his friend. But there was a thought that wouldn't go away: the knowledge that he had once wished for harm to come to Pat, so he would have his chance to claim the mine for himself. This had been the year before, when Hyde and Williams had only recently met, and the mine was solely in Williams's name. Much as he'd needed the silver, Hyde had eventually decided that no amount of money was worth the loss of honour from betraying a man who was proving to be a good friend. But if he could come so close to betraying Pat, it was surely possible that Pat could have betrayed him. Betrayal by Pat was almost impossible to believe, but it was a fact that someone had betrayed the route that the silver delivery would take.

* * *

They accomplished the ride to El Paso without further incident. Hyde's first stop was at the bank, where the remaining silver was safely deposited. With the silver delivered, Hyde took a deep breath, suddenly realizing just how much the responsibility for it had been weighing on him. The men who'd accompanied him had taken the horses and mules to a livery barn while he'd been dealing with the bank, and had then gone off to enjoy themselves around the brothels, dancehalls, saloons, cantinas and gambling dens of the border town. Hyde was on his own, but he was grateful for the solitude. After eating a hearty meal in a quiet restaurant, he made his way to the hotel he usually stayed at. There, he simply set his saddlebags on the floor, and although it was only mid-afternoon, he stretched out on the narrow bed and slept deeply until after supper time.

★　★　★

'They're back!'

McKindrick's call fetched Pat Williams from the bunkhouse, where he'd been whiling away the time before supper with a game of monte with the miners. The Scottish miner was standing in the creek, wearing nothing but a faded kilt, which did little to conceal his knotty muscles and his splendidly hairy torso. McKindrick pointed down the canyon with his left hand, holding a sodden shirt that dripped dirty, soapy water in his right.

'Ah reckon as they're all present an' guid,' he announced cheerfully.

Williams could see the riders approaching for himself. Señor de la Valle's men would have returned to the hacienda, so only Hyde, Esteban and Busby were returning to the mine. They looked relaxed, without the air of defeat that he'd seen the last time. Williams stepped forward eagerly, welcoming them back. He met Hyde as his partner reached the small corral beside the office building. The other two men called greetings as they led the packmules past, heading for the larger corral at the other end of the canyon.

'Is everyone safe?' Williams asked

Hyde, patting Cob's neck as the horse blew at him through velvet nostrils.

Hyde nodded, then swung his leg over to dismount, landing lightly. 'No man so much as scratched,' he reported. 'But they were waiting for us again. We lost a mule and its silver.'

The loss of more silver was a disappointment, but it wasn't the most important thing. 'But no one was hurt?' Williams asked again, wanting reassurance.

Hyde shook his head. 'I saw the ambush before we were right into it. We downed three or four of them, but the only casualty we had was one of the packmules and its load of silver. I got the rest to El Paso and deposited it in the bank.'

He took a slip of paper from the inside pocket of his black jacket and held it out.

Williams took the receipt and glanced at it, looking up again to see Hyde looking at him searchingly. Hyde's expression instantly changed to the inscrutable look he'd often had when they'd first met.

'Is there something wrong?' Williams asked impulsively.

'No,' Hyde answered flatly. He softened the reply with a half-smile, just a slight movement of his mouth. 'I got to see to Cob,' he added, patting the horse's neck.

Williams nodded. 'Supper should be ready in a few minutes. I'm glad you're back safe.' He clapped Hyde on the shoulder and headed back to the bunkhouse.

Losing more silver was a blow, but it could have been worse, Williams felt. He wanted to know more about the attack, but Hyde clearly didn't want to talk about it much. Pat Williams believed that Hyde took the losses as a personal failure. He was in charge of escorting the silver from the mine to El Paso, so the success of the robberies meant that he'd failed in his duty and had been beaten by his enemy. Hyde wasn't the kind of man to accept failure readily, so the robberies no doubt rankled with him more than he wanted to let on. Dealing with his proud, independent friend could be a challenge at times, but Williams valued him all the same. He knew he could trust Hyde, and that was the most important thing of all.

9

The familiar, solemn ceremony of Mass helped free Williams's mind from worries about the mine and concern about Hyde's moods. On Sundays, he attended the little, whitewashed chapel on Señor de la Valle's hacienda. Don Pedro and his daughter sat alone in the family pew, while Williams, his mother and two sisters sat in a place of honour on the other side of the central aisle. Williams surreptitiously glanced sideways at Conchita; her dark eyes were on the priest, her attention on the ritual. She looked lovely as she listened to the reading of the lesson, engrossed in the story. Refreshed by this glimpse of her, Williams turned his own attention back to the service.

After the service, there was lunch in the family house, then they moved to the courtyard to relax and talk. The courtyard at the centre of the main house was a beautiful area, filled with tubs and beds of flowers that scented the air, and with pleasantly shady arbours to escape the heat of the sun. Williams sat in a corner with Conchita, out of sight of everyone except for an elderly aunt who was supposed to be a chaperon. The aunt was sitting a few feet away though, emitting delicate snores as she napped in the afternoon's heat.

Williams took Conchita's dainty hand and smiled lovingly at her.

'Seeing you is a refreshment for me,' he told her in Spanish.

'Good,' she said warmly. 'Costilla told us about the robbery.' Her mood changed as she continued. 'It's so unfair that you do all the work of digging the mine and smelting the silver, then some *banditos* steal it without doing any of the work.'

Williams was touched by her indignation. 'At least no one was hurt this time. Poor Zeke is in El Paso now.

There's no doctor in Hueco, so I sent him on to El Paso, just so's the doctor there could keep an eye on his leg. I've seen bullet wounds go real bad afore. Hyde visited him, and said he's mending nicely.'

'All the same, it is not right,' Conchita said passionately. 'The *banditos* should be hung.'

'They will be, if they don't get shot first,' Williams said. 'Their luck can't hold out for ever.' He paused, and looked at her before speaking again. 'Let's not talk about bad things. Tell me what you've been doing this week. That's a new dress, isn't it?'

Conchita smiled, and stroked the flounced skirt of her black-and-red dress. 'You always notice when I have new things.

'You look so pretty in them.'

'Don't I look pretty in the old things?' she asked, pouting prettily as her eyes sparkled with humour.

'Whatever you wear, you are the prettiest woman I know,' he reassured her.

Conchita smiled tenderly. 'When you say that, it sounds different to when other men call me pretty.'

Pat Williams' answer came readily. 'Because when I say it, I say it with real love.' It was the simple truth. From the moment he'd first, unexpectedly set eyes on her, he'd been bewitched by the lovely, lively generous young woman. They found it easy to make one another laugh; she offered him support in the difficult times and helped him to relax and enjoy himself. They danced together, and she played guitar for him and he read poetry to her. When he was away from her, Pat Williams sometimes found it hard to believe that this delightful woman, daughter of a grand, wealthy family, could love him.

Williams knew that Conchita would inherit the hacienda and ranch, and that her husband would be a wealthy man because of it. All the same, he wanted a suitable income of his own, not least because it smoothed over the social differences between them. He knew that many of Don Pedro's extended family regarded him as an upstart, lacking in decent family and background. The money from the silver mine gave him a social status he'd never have otherwise. The recent robberies threatened not only himself and his ability to look after his mother and sisters, Williams also felt that it threatened his future with Conchita. He was certain that Don Pedro respected him for himself, but he also knew how deeply the notions of honour and society went among the old Spanish families. He couldn't help feeling that if he lost the mine, he would also lose Conchita. And that thought frightened him.

*   *   *

Conchita had confidence in Williams, and said so a couple of days later to her cousin, when Ramon visited.

'He's got a lot of gumption,' she said firmly, switching from Spanish into

English to make her point. 'It took him four years to find the man who stole his father's map of the mine, but he got it back. And he fought off Comanches to keep it.'

Ramon nodded, pulling another grape off the bunch that Conchita had provided for him, knowing how much he loved them. 'He's got courage,' Ramon agreed, in Spanish. 'But many men who have courage fail or die.'

'Pat will make a success of the mine,' Conchita insisted, glaring at her cousin. 'You don't like him because he is an *Anglo*,' she added, obstinately sticking to English. 'But he is not the one who took your family's land. He has taken nothing from the Spanish.'

Ramon shook his head. 'You're wrong, Concepción, I think Williams is a good man. I'm just worried that things are not going well for him and you are to be married in a few months.'

Conchita studied her cousin for a few moments, and felt some of her anger melt. She couldn't help but be amused by some of his conceits, like the way he tried to appear taller than he really was, but he had always been kind to her. She was still fairly certain that he disapproved of her engagement to Pat Williams, but she had been raised to obey the men of her family, and so made no further attempt to contradict him about his attitude to Williams.

Ramon fiddled with the bunch of grapes, eating one absent-mindedly as he stared across the courtyard, frowning slightly.

'What are you thinking about?' Conchita asked.

He looked straight at her, as if making up his mind about something, then spoke. 'I was thinking about the ambushes — that the *banditos* know where and when to wait.'

'Someone is telling them,' Conchita interrupted.

Ramon nodded. 'The only people who know the route in advance are Williams and Hyde. And Hyde is the one who is present when the thieves show up. He is the one who has surrendered to them, and let them take the silver.'

Conchita was shocked into silence for a moment, before the words burst out of her. 'That's . . . Hyde would do no such thing! He's Pat's partner. Pat trusts him completely.'

'A man who trusts can never be betrayed; only mistaken. Maybe Williams is mistaken in his trust of Hyde.'

Conchita shook her head, black hair flying around her face. 'Why would Hyde help someone steal the silver? He didn't help them! He was there in the middle of it, risking his life to help his men escape with the silver. Costilla told me all about it — he saw it!'

Ramon leaned forward in his chair. 'Don't you think it's strange that he never got hurt? He was the one doing most of the shooting; he was the easiest target and the leader. Yet neither Hyde nor his horse have been so much as scratched. With so many men shooting at him, and the kind of range Costillo described, he *should* have been hit. But if he were collaborating with the *banditos*, they would be careful not to shoot him.'

Conchita shook her head again, stunned at what her cousin was suggesting. 'I will not believe that of Hyde. He is a good man. He has saved Pat's life and he saved my life, remember? He has half a share of the mine — why should he steal the silver?'

Ramon gave her a patronizing look. 'My sweet, you have known nothing but comfort and wealth all your life. You don't know how bitter poverty can make a man. Imagine how it must have been for Hyde. He too lived like this.' Ramon gestured at the pretty surroundings. 'He had slaves to do the work and look after him, a family and money. He lost all that in the war and only now, with Williams's silver mine, has he had money again. That taste of money has tempted him, and he wants more. He wants it all.'

Conchita stared at Ramon in dismay,

thinking about what he had said. It was true that Hyde had lost a lot, and only natural that he should wish to be wealthy again. But she didn't want to believe that he was associated with the robberies.

'Hyde is a gentleman,' she said at last. 'He would not betray his partnership with Pat.'

Ramon reached out and placed his hand on hers. 'I'm sorry to shock you, Conchita. I hope I'm wrong. It's the only explanation that makes sense to me, though.'

It made sense to Conchita too, but only in an abstract way. Ramon's suggestion was plausible, but she wouldn't believe that Hyde would actually do such a thing.

'I can't believe you, Ramon,' she said at last. 'I know Hyde better than you and he wouldn't betray Pat. He just wouldn't.' But the idea, once spoken, could not be unspoken.

* * *

Hyde's first stop in Hueco was the teamsters, to see if the chemical supplies ordered for the mine had arrived. Shaw, the owner, told him that they were due in after lunch, so Hyde rode on to the centre of town. He stopped first at the grocery store and gave in his order. The storekeeper, Morris, held the list close to his nose, and scanned it slowly, grunting as he read each item.

'Cain't let ye have but the two pounds of bacon,' he said, spitting the words out jerkily.

'That'll be fine,' Hyde drawled. 'Is there anything else?'

'You want Arbuckle's coffee, or beans? Beans are cheaper.'

'Arbuckle's,' Hyde answered firmly.

Morris nodded, and squinted at his customer. 'I got everything else.'

'I'll be in town another couple of hours,' Hyde said. 'There's no call to load the mules now, I'll pick up the goods when I'm ready to leave town.'

Morris nodded and turned away,

weaving his way between the barrels of goods, piles of buckets, clusters of butter churns and other things that cluttered the floor, while still studying the list. How he managed to cross the store without knocking anything over was a mystery to Hyde. He watched in wonder for a moment, then turned and left.

With business taken care of, he could relax and enjoy the visit to town. Hueco's mix of simply-made adobe and lumber buildings, most only single-storey, hardly compared to cities like Charleston. However, it was positively grand after spending days at the isolated mine. And, limited though the amenities were, they offered luxuries he couldn't get in the canyon.

Hyde's next stop was the mercantile store, for a new shirt of dark grey cotton, and new socks. He could have bought similar items a little more cheaply from Morris's store, but he knew from experience that clothes from the general store were permeated with the mingled aromas of cheese, tobacco, kerosene, salt fish and coffee that characterized such places. Although his first intention had been to buy just the plain clothes, he found himself looking at pairs of *calzoneras*. The dark-green pair he'd worn to the *fiesta* had been borrowed from Diaz, Señor de la Valle's *segundo*. Now he saw a blue pair, with a narrow red stripe and silver buttons along the outer seam, that appealed to him. As he held them against himself, he realized that something inside him was changing.

Since the end of the war, his clothing had all been functional, and mostly black or grey. He'd been in mourning for both his father and younger brother, of course, as well as all the cousins and other relatives who'd died in the war. But he'd also been in mourning for the end of the life he'd always known. He'd worn brighter clothes back before the war. Hyde had never been a dandy, but he'd dressed up for balls and barbecues and took a pride in being well turned-out. That gracious plantation life had been swept away, leaving him adrift.

He'd been a partner in the mine for nearly a year now, but only in the last couple of months had he felt the desire to dress up again, and wear colours. The bleakness of the post-war years was giving way to a prosperous future. And when he thought of the future, he wanted Queenie there with him. Hyde looked at the trousers and smiled to himself. Queenie's porcelain beauty deserved a well-dressed gentleman and he wanted to show her that he fitted that role. Hyde added the colourful *calzoneras* to the practical clothes he'd chosen.

With fresh clothing under his arm, he crossed the street to the barber's. There, he indulged in a good soak in a hot bath, before sitting back in the leather-padded chair for a haircut and shave. When the barber was done, Hyde inspected himself carefully in the mirror before settling his faded black hat over his dark hair, and heading back out into the sunshine.

He paused on the sidewalk, relishing the sensation of being properly clean and well turned-out. Sunlight sparkled on the silver buttons of the *calzoneras* he was now wearing. Hyde felt fit to be in civilized company again, even if it was just this dusty little town. It was close to time for the noon meal, and there were fewer people about than when he'd arrived. Hyde indulged himself in watching the citizens of Hueco for a few moments, intending to mount up and ride over to the Williams's house. As he glanced about, a sharp movement caught his eye.

Battle-honed reflexes kicked in, and Hyde turned swiftly to see a Mexican about forty yards away, staring at him in shock. He didn't recognize the man, who was completely average in height and clothing. The stranger had clearly recognized him, however; his attitude rigid with alarm. As Hyde stared back, the Mexican's hand twitched towards his gun, then he turned and fled.

When he saw the man's hand move, Hyde drew his own revolver from pure reflex, but he held his fire as the man spun round and sprinted away. Shoving the gun back into its holster, he freed Cob's reins with the other hand. Hyde vaulted aboard and whirled his horse round on its back legs. Cob sprang forward into a gallop as Hyde was still finding his stirrups. He didn't know why the stranger had fled from him, but it seemed like a good idea to find out.

As Cob raced along the near-empty street, Hyde drew his Colt again. The running man threw a glance back over his shoulder, and saw Hyde chasing him. He leapt for the saddle of a range horse tethered to the hitching rail outside the cantina. The brown horse threw up its head and snorted as the rider landed unexpectedly on its back. The Mexican leaned forward to free the reins, and spurred his horse into a gallop.

Hyde went after him but made no

attempt to fire yet. He was confident in his ability to score a hit, but there was always the chance of something going wrong, and he didn't want to take the risk of hitting a bystander unless absolutely necessary. Dust rose in the street as the two horses raced for the edge of town. Hyde leaned forward in his saddle, watching the man ahead of him. The stranger glanced over his shoulder a couple of times, but otherwise sat quietly in his saddle, keeping his horse going at a good speed. A small dog ran into the street and chased the Mexican's horse, yapping shrilly. A boy dashed out after it, realized Hyde was coming straight at him, and threw himself backwards. Hyde caught a glimpse of the boy falling, his arms windmilling, as Cob thundered past. The horse put in a long, jumping stride to be sure of clearing the boy, and settled smoothly back into his regular gallop.

Cob's ears flicked back at a word of praise from his master, then pricked forwards again as he continued to chase the other horse. The little dog was soon left behind and the riders were reaching the end of the street. At this end of town, the businesses gave way to a few scattered shacks. Beyond them was the high desert land. Hyde wondered where the Mexican hoped to flee to. He was unlikely to get so far ahead that he could lose his pursuer. The wild ride confirmed Hyde's first thought that the Mexican had simply panicked, and was fleeing blindly. Why he'd panicked was another matter; a guilty conscience seemed the most likely reason, and Hyde suddenly had an idea. The stranger was probably one of the bandits who had ambushed him and stolen the silver. With that thought, it became all the more important to catch the man and ask him a few questions. Hyde dug his heels into Cob's side, and the horse lengthened its stride, starting to catch the rider ahead.

10

The Mexican glanced back over his shoulder, and saw that Hyde was closer than before. Hyde saw his eyes widen, then the man turned back. Hyde drew his gun, expecting an attack, but the Mexican did something else. He swerved his horse in a dirt-scattering turn, leaving the trail to head across the wild country. Hyde followed, moving at a less dramatic angle as he gave chase. They were heading for the rougher ground, with its hazards of arroyos and rocks.

The Mexican was lashing his horse with the ends of his reins, urging it to greater effort. Hyde encouraged Cob with his legs and his voice; he wore spurs, but Cob didn't need them. Hyde let Cob pick his own path between the rocks and shrubs that littered the desert. The long whips of ocotillo branches snatched at them as they thundered past. The brown horse ahead hesitated, then sprang forward, losing momentum. Hyde sat a little tighter in his saddle, scanning the ground ahead. Moments later he saw the gash in the earth that crossed their path. The crack was some eight feet wide; on foot it would have been impossible to risk, but he knew his horse could do it easily. Hyde took a closer feel of the reins, alerting his horse to an obstacle ahead. Cob lengthened his stride as they approached, and flew over smoothly.

They were even closer now. As Hyde drew one of his guns, the Mexican glanced back and saw him arm himself. He hauled on his reins, changing direction away from Hyde with a shower of dirt. Hyde switched direction less sharply, losing some of the ground he'd gained, but putting less strain on his horse's legs. Hyde ended up behind the fleeing man, and off to one side, riding parallel to him. Cob galloped on steadily, ears pricked and his flaxen mane rising and falling with his stride.

The Mexican's horse was running evenly too, showing no signs of being tired yet. This chase could go on for some time, and Hyde didn't want that. There was a rock outcropping ahead, and he had to choose whether to swerve to pass the same side as his quarry, and lose ground, or whether to keep to his course and delay his opportunity to shoot.

He opted to stay on the path he was following, passing to the left of the rock. It forced him slightly further away from the Mexican's path, but the desert was pretty open, and Hyde had confidence that he wouldn't lose the man. Sure enough, the Mexican was easy to see once Hyde cleared the rock. He was now some eighty feet to Hyde's right. To Hyde's surprise, the Mexican brought his horse to an abrupt halt. As horse and man peered downwards, Hyde realized that they must be on the edge of an arroyo. The brown horse hesitated, taking a step back, then at a kick from its rider, stepped over the edge. It lurched forward and disappeared down the slope.

Now he knew it was there, Hyde could pick out the edge of the arroyo as he galloped towards it. Holstering his gun, he sat tight in the saddle and collected his horse, preparing them for the obstacle. Cob was trotting when they reached the edge of the arroyo, where he halted, snorting. The side of the arroyo here was a near-vertical drop of some twenty feet: from Cob's back, it looked even further. The slope was less steep at the point where the Mexican had gone down, eighty feet away. The Mexican had turned in Hyde's direction though, and was now galloping along the dry arroyo almost under where Hyde was now. Riding to the shallower slope would lose him too much ground.

He made his decision in a split second, and nudged his horse forward. Cob put his front feet over the edge, then backed up, snorting.

'Come on,' Hyde urged, pressing

harder with his legs.

Cob stepped forward again, peering down the slope with his ears flickering back and forth. As Hyde kept urging him forward, the horse stepped over the edge. Terrifying though it was, Hyde didn't lean back, but kept slightly forward in his saddle. The ground below seemed to rush up at them. Cob's forelegs were extended straight in front of him, his back legs tucked underneath himself so he was almost sitting on his tail as he slid down the arroyo wall. Hyde's stomach swooped as they plummeted down, loose stones and dirt cascading around them as Cob's hoofs tore strips of earth away. It was frightening and exhilarating at the same time.

Five feet from the bottom and still sliding, Cob jumped away from the slope. Balanced over the horse's withers, Hyde stayed with him as he kicked out. They landed several feet clear of the slope, Cob's momentum taking him straight into a canter. He came back to hand in two strides, turning and racing after the Mexican, who was now just thirty feet away and straight ahead. In spite of the situation, Hyde was grinning with pleasure at his success in tackling the arroyo wall. He clapped his horse on the neck, then drew his Colt again, concentrating as he aimed.

The arroyo was narrow, the sides here far too steep for a horse to climb. The Mexican had no choice but to ride straight along it. There was nowhere for him to dodge now. He urged his horse on with spurs and lashes of the reins, but it couldn't outrun Cob. Hyde's first shot missed, though the Mexican flinched. He panicked, drew his own gun and screwed around in his saddle, attempting to shoot the man behind him. Hyde moved Cob slightly to the left, aimed and fired again. The Mexican's back arched as the shot ploughed through the back of his shoulder. He dropped the reins from a suddenly limp arm, and slumped to the left. He might have been all right if his spooked horse hadn't shied off to its right. Already off-balance, the Mexican tumbled from his horse.

He hit the sandy dirt, but his left foot was jammed in the wide stirrup. The brown horse continued to run, dragging him along the arroyo floor. Hyde heard a cry of pain and knew the horse's iron-shod hoofs had hit the bandit at least once. He holstered his gun and urged Cob even faster, swinging right to come up alongside the brown. The brown started bucking and fly-jumping, trying to rid itself of the limp thing hanging from its side and getting under its feet. Hyde had no time to see if it was kicking the bandit; he was concentrating on getting close enough to catch it.

Leaning from his saddle, and making soothing sounds, Hyde managed to catch one of the trailing reins.

'Whoa there. Whoa, boy,' he said, slowing Cob and the brown with him.

Reassured by his presence, the brown quickly slowed. As it did, the limp body it dragged became less frightening, and Hyde rapidly had it under control. When the two blowing horses finally stopped Hyde dismounted. Leaving Cob's reins dangling, he approached the brown and spoke calmly to it. When the horse's ears pricked forward, Hyde patted it on the neck. It shook itself vigorously, then snorted and relaxed.

'Good boy,' Hyde said calmly. Reassured that the horse would stand, he moved round to free the bandit's foot from the stirrup, letting it fall to the ground. Pushing the horse gently to one side, Hyde knelt down to examine the man he'd been chasing.

The bandit was dead, his skull caved in by at least two blows from his horse's hoofs. Hyde grunted in annoyance; he'd shot to wound rather than kill, because he'd wanted to talk to the man. He wanted to know why the Mexican had fled from him in town. Hyde searched the body, finding the usual items, like a few cigarillos in a cheap steel case, a folding knife, a grubby handkerchief and some coins. More interestingly, he found a fancy leather billfold stuffed with notes. Hyde counted seventy-four dollars; far more than a regular hacienda worker earned in two months.

'This your pay for stealing our silver?' Hyde asked the corpse. 'I'll swear all ways you'd didn't come by this much honestly. And if you won it at cards, I bet you cheated.'

A corpse with a billfold and no money at all might arouse suspicion. Hyde put sixty-eight dollars in his own pocket-book, leaving six in the Mexican's. He'd give the money to Pat later, to go in the mine's bank account. Thinking of Pat Williams, Hyde suddenly remembered that he was expected to dinner in town. Cursing the dead man, he heaved the corpse up into the saddle of the brown and lashed it there with leather ties. Then he remounted Cob, picked up the brown's rein and set about finding a place where they could get out of the arroyo.

Hyde was back in the mine office, sorting through the receipts, when Williams entered. Pat Williams was fresh from working down the mine, and wore his shirt open and untucked, showing the slight paunch he carried in spite of the hard work he did.

He greeted Hyde, and asked, 'Did you get all the chemicals?'

'All arrived safe,' Hyde reassured him. 'They're over in the smelting house. Got the rest of the stores too.'

'Good.' Williams dropped into the chair on the other side of the desk, giving a sigh of relief.

Hyde looked at his sweaty, dishevelled friend, and felt slightly guilty about his own well-groomed appearance. He'd ridden miles and done a useful job of work today, but it didn't seem quite the same as labouring with a pickaxe down the mine.

'How was dinner with Momma and the girls?' Williams asked.

'Your mother's a fine cook,' Hyde drawled. 'And she's surely got a way of making a place into a real home. I felt plumb honoured to visit with them.'

Williams smiled happily. 'They're good company, ain't they?' He chuckled. 'Though I guess Caitlin hardly stopped talking the whole time; she's a regular chatterbox.'

'That's so.'

'I'm glad Queenie and Conchita get on so well,' Williams went on contentedly. 'They were talking at the picnic, iffen you recall. Conchita tells me they go riding sometimes, and Queenie's been visiting a couple of times. I was hoping Conchita and my family would like one another, so I'm real made up that she and Queenie are friends. Queenie doesn't talk as much as Caitlin, but when she does, she talks sense. What did you make of her?' Williams added.

'I . . . ' Hyde stumbled for an answer. Sitting at table with Queenie had been a bitter-sweet experience. To be in her presence, to look at her and listen to her, had been a delight. But all the time he'd been on guard against revealing the way he felt about her. He'd wanted to talk to her with the same warmth and freedom as when they'd been riding, but it wasn't possible in front of her mother and sister. Hyde looked at Williams, wondering if he dared tell him the truth yet. Pat's face was open, interested in what Hyde was saying. But Hyde still had no idea how he would react to the idea of his partner courting his youngest sister, and was scared to ask in case the idea was vetoed. 'I like Queenie,' he said awkwardly.

Williams gave him a puzzled look. 'Well, I'm sure they were glad to have company,' he said. 'Anything happen in town?'

Hyde started to shake his head, occupied with thoughts of Queenie and her family, then suddenly remembered.

'Why, yes.' He told Williams about the stranger who had recognized him and fled, and the chase. 'I took the body to the marshal in town,' he finished. 'He said he'd telegraph Sheriff Hill and get him to look at the body, see if he could match him to any wanted notices.'

Williams scratched his head. 'I reckon you're right. He knew who you were and must have thought you'd recognize him too. If he hadn't done panicked and run, you probably wouldn't have given him a second glance. It sure was lucky for us, if the sheriff can identify him. If he can, he might be able to track down more of those thieves, and maybe our silver.'

'I got this off him,' Hyde said, remembering. He produced the sixty-eight dollars from his pocketbook and leaned across the table to give it to Williams. 'I figured it was most likely his payment for stealing from us, so I reckoned we had as much title to it as anyone.'

Williams looked at the wad of notes. 'I'm not sure the marshal would say that's legal,' he remarked. 'But I reckon you've got a point. And what's done is done.' He passed the money back again. 'Put it in the safe now, and it can go in the bank next time one of us goes to El Paso.'

Hyde stood and crossed to the corner of the room where the safe stood. He put the money inside and locked it again, then turned to see Williams staring at him with a look of surprise.

'Is something wrong?' Hyde asked self-consciously.

Williams shook his head, his blue eyes sparkling. 'I didn't know you'd gone and got yourself all gussied up.' He pointed to Hyde's legs.

Hyde glanced down, and realized he was wearing the new calzoneras. He assumed a casual air as he moved back to the desk. 'I reckoned as I needed new clothes for visiting.'

'They look swell,' Williams said. He leaned back in his chair and stretched. 'I'm gonna get me a good wash before supper.' He rose and headed for his bedroom at the back of the office building.

Hyde picked up his pen. 'I'll finish entering these receipts in the books and tally up.'

Williams grinned. 'I'm sure glad one of us can do maths.' He vanished into his room to fetch his washing kit.

Hyde stared blankly at the account book for a moment, remembering Queenie sitting at the table, her green eyes looking at him with warmth. Shaking his head, he got back to work.

11

Two days later, it was Pat William's turn to get away from the mine for a while. He went first to Hueco, to get himself spruced up, and visit his family, then, after the noontime dinner, he rode on to the Casa de las Flores, to visit with Conchita. They sat in the shade of the courtyard, the scent of many flowers filling the warm air. Williams gazed happily at Conchita, so delicate and feminine in her ruffled yellow dress. They talked for a while about life at the hacienda, and she made him laugh with an account of chickens getting into the vegetable garden and wreaking havoc there. In return, he told her about Hyde's encounter with the stranger in Hueco.

She looked at him thoughtfully, fiddling with one of the ruffles on her wide skirt.

'It seems strange that the bandit should run away like that,' she said.

'I guess he panicked,' Williams replied.

'But Señor Hyde, he insists that he didn't recognize the man?'

'Well, the bandits all had bandannas drawn up over their faces, so he didn't get to see them very well.' Williams frowned slightly. 'You seem worried about something, sweetheart?'

Conchita fidgeted some more. 'What if Hyde did recognize him?' she asked quietly.

Williams was puzzled by the suggestion, but thought about it. 'If Hyde *did* know the bandit, why would he chase him and shoot him? And why would he lie about not knowing him?'

Conchita looked up, her dark eyes wide. 'Ramon . . . he thinks Hyde is working with the bandits to steal the silver.' The words began spilling out of her, faster and faster. 'Hyde tells them the route, so they know where to put the ambush. And although he's been fighting, he hasn't been hurt because they don't shoot at him. They are missing him deliberately. Maybe when Hyde saw the bandit in Hueco, he didn't want the risk that the bandit would tell anyone that Hyde had paid him, so Hyde chased him and killed him.'

'He didn't shoot to kill,' Williams said. 'It's not his fault the man got dragged and trampled.'

Conchita shrugged, looking distressed.

'And Hyde has a half-share of the mine,' Williams went on, beginning to get angry. 'Why should he team up with some *banditos* to steal silver that's half his anyway? I don't believe he'd betray me like that!' Looking at the miserable Conchita, he took a deep breath. 'You don't really believe it either, do you?' he said more quietly.

She shook her head. 'Señor Hyde is a good, brave man. I don't like to think that he would do such a thing.'

'Your cousin, Ramon, doesn't know Hyde, and he doesn't know what he's talking about,' Williams said flatly.

Picking up his drink, he leaned back in his chair and thought about his partner. He liked and trusted Hyde, and it had never once occurred to him that his partner might be involved in the robberies. Although both Hyde and Williams had served in the war, Hyde had more combat experience and was the better horseman and gunman of the two. It had seemed logical for him to take charge of escorting the silver bullion to the bank. Yet while all Williams's instincts denied the possibility of Hyde betraying him, one thing stood out. The ambushers had known exactly where and when to strike. *Somebody* from the mine was giving them the information, and Williams knew it wasn't himself.

'Do you trust your cousin, Ramon?' he asked Conchita, unconsciously switching from Spanish back into English.

'Of course,' she answered, somewhat startled. 'I have known him all my life. He's always been kind to me.'

'And do you trust Hyde?'

She lifted her hands in a helpless gesture. 'Yes. Until now I've trusted him like I trust you.'

'You don't trust him now?'

'I don't know what to think!' she exclaimed, lapsing back into her native Spanish. 'He's a good and brave man. He has saved your life, and mine and he is a gentleman. But Ramon said maybe Señor Hyde wants to be rich again, like he was before the war, and that's why he wants all of the silver.'

The last remark caught Pat Williams off guard. He knew of Hyde's background, of course, and when they'd first taken over the mine, he'd realized how hard it was for Hyde to accustom himself to his new role. Since then Hyde had seemed to settle down. Williams realized somewhat guiltily that, absorbed in his own happiness with Conchita, he'd assumed that Hyde was content too. Williams thought back, trying to pinpoint any warning signs.

Of course, Hyde had been unwilling

to talk about the first ambush. Williams had assumed it was because he'd felt ashamed at the loss of the silver but now another explanation occurred to him: Hyde could have been concealing guilt over arranging the theft of the silver. Williams suddenly remembered the day Hyde had gone for a long ride and not got back until after supper. He'd rejected the offer of company, and had been evasive about what he'd been up to. Williams had dismissed his partner's doings as none of his business, but perhaps he should be concerned after all. It was after those hours spent away from the mine, doing something he didn't want to talk about, that Hyde had led the silver straight into the second ambush.

Williams shook his head. 'It's all coincidence and rumour,' he said, looking across the table at Conchita. 'Please don't tell anyone else what Ramon said. Hyde would be mighty upset if he found out.' Williams shook his head again. 'I won't believe it of him.' Because believing that his friend and partner had betrayed him was too painful for Williams to bear.

★　★　★

Williams left the bunkhouse, stepping out of the smoky air into the fresher, cool air of the canyon at dusk. He hadn't been able to concentrate on the poker game with McKindrick, Busby and Goras, so had opted to quit, and take a wander in the peace outside. His thoughts were still unsettled after his talk with Conchita the day before. Williams turned to look at the office building, which had his room and Hyde's at the back. Hyde was sitting on the bench in front of the building. He was holding a book, but not reading it. Instead, he had his head leaning back against the wall behind him, and was gazing up towards the stars.

Williams walked slowly towards him, his boots quiet on the packed dirt path between the buildings.

177

'Hyde?'

Hyde started, almost dropping the book as his right hand twitched towards his hip. He wasn't wearing his gunbelt, but the movement was instinctive. Recollecting himself, he closed the book and looked at Williams.

'What were you thinking about?' Williams asked impulsively.

Hyde's expression changed briefly, to what Williams felt sure was a look of guilt, then his face became firmly neutral.

'Nothing,' Hyde said abruptly. He hesitated, then added. 'I was thinking of going to El Paso. I can put that cash from the bandit in the bank, and visit Zeke, see how he's getting on.'

'We haven't enough bullion yet to make another trip worthwhile,' Williams said, watching Hyde's face intently.

'I wasn't thinking of taking bullion,' Hyde drawled, his grey eyes narrowing as he looked back at Williams. 'Though I could carry three or four bars in my saddlebags. I don't reckon anyone would be waiting for me travelling alone.'

The suggestion made sense, but Williams couldn't help but wonder if it were an excuse for Hyde to do what he liked with the silver, with no witnesses. He shook his head, dismissing the idea and trying to dispel his own suspicion.

'I . . . I reckon the silver's safe enough here, for now,' he replied. 'When were you reckoning on going to El Paso?' he asked, not really interested, but trying to make a regular conversation.

'In a couple days.'

Williams nodded. 'I figured on going to Hueco tomorrow to visit with Momma and the girls, maybe see if Queenie wants to go out for a ride. You could go to El Paso a couple of days later?'

He couldn't make out Hyde's expression. It was too still, almost concealing his partner's thoughts, but Williams could tell that Hyde was uncomfortable about something he'd mentioned.

'You want to go to El Paso a particular day?' he asked.

Hyde shook his head sharply. 'I don't care too hard when I go.' He stood up suddenly, the movement graceful, and turned to leave.

'Hyde.'

'What?' The question was snapped curtly as Hyde looked back at Williams.

Pat Williams didn't know what he wanted to ask; he'd just spoken because he was sure that his friend was keeping something from him. He couldn't bring himself to ask the question he really wanted, instead asking:

'Are you sure you don't know who's involved in stealing the silver?'

Hyde's eyes widened briefly. 'I don't know anything about the damn silver,' he said flatly. Turning on his heel, he stalked away to the mouth of the canyon.

Williams watched him go, not sure whether he'd hurt his friend, or was being betrayed by him.

★ ★ ★

Hyde was relieved by the sight of El Paso as he rode towards the town. He had things to do in the town, and hopefully there would be opportunities to turn his mind outwards, and forget the problems he'd been brooding over during his solitary ride. The foremost issue was telling Pat how he felt about Queenie. She fascinated and entranced him; she was beautiful, and easy company, and she could make him laugh. Hyde knew that if he wanted to spend more time with her, even, as he hoped, to marry her, he would have to be open about his feelings for her.

He feared though, that Pat would disapprove. Hyde was, after all, thirteen years older than Queenie, and was not a Catholic. And he was certain that Queenie would not go against the wishes of her family. But the guilt of their secret meetings, of lying to Pat, was too much for him. In any case, Pat clearly suspected that he was lying about something, and that suspicion could easily lead to discord. It was better to confess than to be caught out. As he rode into town, Hyde tried to push those thoughts aside.

The livery stable he normally used was full, so he took the owner's recommendation and made his way to another stable, in a part of town he was less familiar with. The smell of horses, leather and clean straw was good, and a look about reassured him that the place was up to his standards. Hyde settled Cob in a roomy stall, and left him with a bucket of clean water and a feed of good oats. Cob buried his muzzle in the manger, and ate contentedly. Hyde lingered in the stall for a moment, enjoying the soothing sound of steady eating. He patted his horse on the rump as he walked out.

'At least you're not worried about the future,' he drawled.

Walking through the stable, Hyde naturally looked about at the other animals there. A light-grey coat stood out in the lower light of the thick adobe building. Looking with more attention,

Hyde realized the grey was a mule, not a horse. Grey mules were uncommon, and he turned to look more closely. There wasn't much to distinguish it from any other grey mule, but it looked the same height and build as the one which had been stolen, along with its load of silver, in the first robbery. Hyde cautiously let himself into the stall, speaking to the mule, which twitched its long ears in his direction.

'Easy there,' Hyde said, sliding one hand along the mule's side.

The mule looked at him with large, mild eyes, but Hyde knew from bitter experience that mules kick often, fast, and with tremendous accuracy. He patted the mule again, and examined the brand on its left hip. The mine's mule had been bought from Don Pedro's Casa de las Flores, and had had the hacienda's complicated brand on it. This mule had an even more complicated brand, but as Hyde looked, he could see the basic shape of the hacienda's brand. Touching the brand carefully, he could feel that the extra marks had a different texture from Don Pedro's brand, as though they had been added at a different time. He looked the mule over carefully again, and was as sure as he could be that this was the stolen mule.

Leaving the mule to its hay net, Hyde made his way to the office at the front of the stables. He hung up his saddle and bridle, and paid for Cob's stall, telling Tomas, the livery-barn owner, the name of the stable that had sent him. He complimented Tomas on his stables and introduced himself.

'We need a couple more mules for the mine,' Hyde drawled, standing in a relaxed pose. 'I was admiring that grey mule back there.'

'He's all wool and a yard wide,' Tomas said contentedly, speaking around the thin, unlit cigarette that seemed permanently attached to his mouth. 'I'll hire him to you, but he ain't for sale.'

'Oh.' Hyde sounded disappointed. 'I'd taken a shine to the grey. Have you had him a long time then?'

Tomas shook his head. 'Got him 'bout a month ago. He ain't mean, as mules go, so I'd rather have him in the stables than another.'

Hyde nodded: the first robbery, when the mule had been stolen, had happened about a month ago. 'I like a mule that's good to handle, if I can find one,' he added wryly. Keeping his real feelings hidden, he asked the important question. 'Where did you get him from?'

'Someone came in with three mules for sale. He said his cousin had been using them as pack animals, but done had an accident, and give up his business running packmules to carry goods out to mines and remote places. So he was selling the mules for his cousin. I don't reckon he's got any mules to sell now.'

Three mules had been taken from the silver caravan; Hyde was sure he was on the right track here, but couldn't allow himself to seem too eager. He had no real proof that the mule had belonged to the mine, and Tomas might act awkward if told that his mule was stolen.

Hyde shrugged casually. 'It can't hurt to ask him. What was his name?'

Tomas frowned, sucking on the unlit cigarette. 'Now, he wasn't some common *vaquero*, he was a *rico* — he was a gentleman like you.' He pondered for a moment, then reached across the small table next to his chair, and pulled a sheaf of papers from an old coffee tin. Tomas examined the papers slowly, his lips moving slightly as he read each one.

'Here.' He held out a receipt written on a page torn from an exercise book.

It was a bill of sale for three mules. Hyde could see at once that it had the handwriting of an educated man. The date was three days after the first silver caravan had been ambushed, and the name on the paper was Ramon J F Morales. Hyde turned the paper over, studying it.

'Morales wrote this, right?' he asked.

'Was this his paper?'

Tomas nodded, uncurious. 'Tore it out of this writing book he had with him.'

Hyde would have liked to keep the receipt, but couldn't think of a reason to ask for it. Instead he handed it back, telling to Tomas to take good care of it.

'I'm mighty obliged to you for the help,' he drawled.

'*De nada*,' Tomas replied, sucking on the thin cigarette.

Hyde nodded to him and walked out, fighting down a grin. At last, he could start to fight back against the thieves. And once they were taken care of, he could turn his attention to telling Pat how he felt about Queenie.

12

The next morning, Ramon Morales told Pat Williams that he'd found the stolen silver hidden in a cave.

'You saw Hyde's horse here three weeks ago?' Williams asked him. Williams, Ramon and Conchita had ridden out to a canyon to the east of Hueco, where the cave was. The cave was a natural one, with a shallow creek flowing from the mouth, almost dried up at this time of year.

'I am certain it was Señor Hyde's horse, though I didn't think anything of it at the time,' Ramon replied. He knew that Williams was fluent in Spanish, but spoke English when talking to him. Williams was an *Anglo* and didn't deserve the dignity of using Spanish. 'It was a liver chestnut, with flaxen mane and tail, and a white snip. I couldn't see a brand.'

The description certainly matched Cob; even the lack of a brand was correct.

'I didn't know you rode out this way often,' Conchita said, looking at her cousin.

'I have fond memories of this place,' he replied, smiling at her. 'You remember how we all used to play here? You and the other girls used the cave to play keeping house.'

Conchita nodded, and looked back towards the cave.

Williams dismounted and tethered his brown horse to a juniper bush. He removed a candle from his saddle-bag and set it in a holder. Ramon dismounted gracefully, and helped Conchita down.

'You say it was three weeks ago?' Williams asked, pausing outside the cave to light the candle He stared at Ramon, trying to read the man's handsome face. Ramon nodded.

'It was a couple of days after the full moon. I was here in the late afternoon.'

Williams thought back: Ramon's words confirmed his suspicions. 'I remember he went out for a long ride about then,' Williams said, mostly to himself. 'Didn't want company and never said where he went. He acted kind of funny about it.'

Williams had trusted Hyde, but now so much seemed to indicate that his friend, the man he'd gifted half his hard-won mine to, had stabbed him in the back. The sense of hurt tightened his stomach, and made him feel sick. So much about what Hyde had been doing lately seemed doubtful. Even buying the *calzonares* raised questions. Was Hyde spending more on clothes because he had the extra money from stolen silver? They'd worked and fought together in order to win and keep the mine, but that was last year. Had Hyde's loyalty shifted now that Williams was the only person between himself and full ownership? Williams didn't want to believe it, but he couldn't stop himself from thinking about it. Because, worst of all, even worse than being betrayed by his friend, if he lost the mine he could lose Conchita. That fear made him vulnerable.

Almost reluctantly, he followed Ramon into the cave. The sunlight from outside lit the cave almost to the back, where gloom descended. They made their way past a bulge of rock and into a narrow passage that was low enough to make the men duck their heads, though neither was tall. The candle cast a flickering yellow light that made the passage ahead seem even darker, but Ramon walked on confidently. They walked for a minute or so, the passage twisting and turning as they passed a couple of small side openings. Williams glanced over his shoulder and saw Conchita behind him, her dark eyes glittering in the candlelight. She smiled at him.

'The boys wouldn't let me down here when I was a girl,' she said.

'The cavern is just around this corner,' Ramon told them.

Sure enough, a few moments later, they emerged into a larger cavern, where the creek pooled to one side. Gleaming in the candlelight were bars of silver bullion, neatly stacked in piles. Williams crouched to examine the silver, seeing the familiar, slight imperfections left by the moulds used at his mine.

'This is from the Two Moccasins mine,' he said quietly. 'It looks to be about all that was taken.'

Conchita put her hand on his arm, her eyes sorrowful. 'The silver is not lost. That is good news, at least,' she said.

Williams nodded. 'I guess so.' He sighed, and sagged a little; he felt as though someone had settled lead weights around his shoulders.

Emerging into the sun a few minutes later, Williams stowed a couple of the silver bars into his saddlebag, then helped Conchita to mount again.

'Hyde should be back from El Paso this afternoon,' he told the other two.

'I'm going straight back to the mine to wait for him. You'll see Conchita safely back home, won't you?' he asked Ramon.

'My greatest wish is to see that she is looked after properly,' Ramon answered, standing straight-backed and tall as he faced Williams.

As Williams mounted, Conchita moved her horse over to his.

'Don't be too hasty,' she pleaded, her sweet face anxious.

Williams looked at the mouth of the cave where his silver had been hidden. 'I have to get at the truth,' he answered slowly. 'I need to know the truth.'

*   *   *

Hyde didn't go directly to the mine, riding instead to the Casa de las Flores. He asked for Conchita, and was shown through to the courtyard, where she was sitting at a table with Queenie. Hyde stared at Queenie for a moment, the feelings of longing and guilt rising for a few moments, before he got himself under control. She smiled calmly at him, her slanted green eyes warm with pleasure.

'Good afternoon, Miss Concepción, Miss Queenie,' he drawled, sitting down.

While Queenie looked as collected as usual, Conchita was looking at him anxiously and fidgeting with the ruffles on her skirt. She recollected her manners sufficiently to offer refreshments and managed a wide smile that didn't quite reach her eyes.

Queenie broke the nervous silence. 'Did you have a good time in El Paso?' she asked. 'How's Zeke?'

'Getting fat and sassy,' Hyde said. 'He reckons he'll be back at work next week.'

A servant appeared and set down a tall glass of fresh lemonade, some bread and cheese, and a bunch of red grapes. Hyde took a long, grateful drink of the lemonade, letting Conchita top up his glass afterwards.

'I discovered something interesting in El Paso,' he drawled, studying Conchita. 'You have a cousin Ramon, don't you?'

Conchita nodded, puzzled. 'Sure, he's about somewhere if . . . ' She turned to look for a servant to summon Ramon.

Hyde held up a hand. 'I don't want to see him right now. I want to talk to you first.'

Queenie straightened. 'I think I should be leaving.'

'No,' Hyde said impulsively, looking at her. 'I'd like you to stay,' he added.

She smiled and relaxed again.

'Do I recall correctly that your cousin's name is Ramon Morales?' Hyde asked Conchita.

'Ramon Jose Felipe Morales,' she replied.

Part of Hyde wanted to smile. When he'd seen the name on the receipt at the livery barn, he had quickly remembered meeting Conchita's cousin. He hadn't been sure of the full name, but after the way Conchita's brother had tried to steal the mine, Hyde hadn't been too surprised that another relative might have the same idea. He couldn't be jubilant about making the connection though, for it would mean another member of the family being proved dishonest, and the disgrace of Conchita's now-dead brother had been hard enough.

Gently, he explained about recognizing the mule, and seeing Ramon's name on the receipt. Conchita's expression changed from anxiety to dismay, and she shook her head as Hyde spoke.

'It can't be Ramon!' she protested helplessly. 'Why would he do such a thing?'

'I guess he wants to bankrupt the mine, and buy it up himself,' Hyde said, looking at Queenie for support. She frowned, drumming her fingers on the table before speaking.

'Ramon has accused you of stealing the silver,' she said, looking him straight in the eyes. 'He says you set up the ambushes with the thieves, and kept the silver yourself.'

Hyde simply gaped at her for a moment. 'Why . . . the lying . . . ' He choked off a curse. 'How dare he accuse me of cheating Pat? You can't possibly believe him.'

'He showed us where the silver is hidden,' Conchita said miserably. 'He said he'd seen your horse outside the cave.'

'What cave? When was I supposed to have been there?' Hyde demanded, fighting down the urge to slam his fist on the table.

Conchita shook her head in distress. 'I don't remember. About three weeks ago.'

'Three weeks.' Hyde leaned forward. 'Please, try to remember what he said.'

Conchita frowned, concentrating. 'Ramon said it was just after the full moon; a day or two after, I can't remember. And Pat said you'd been out for a long ride on your own, and he didn't know where you'd been.'

Queenie's eyes widened. 'That would be about the time we went out riding.'

Conchita looked from one to another, startled.

'Miss Queenie and I went for a ride together,' Hyde confessed. 'Her horse stumbled and near-on pulled off its shoe, so we were late getting back.' He paused. 'I didn't dare tell Pat I was out riding with his sister. I just didn't dare tell him that Queenie and I . . . well . . . ' He looked at Queenie, who smiled reassuringly at him. 'I was worried Pat might not like it.'

Conchita smiled with real warmth for the first time since Hyde had joined them. 'I think it's romantic, and I'm sure Pat wants his sisters to be happy. And even if he didn't like it, I'd tell him to shut up.'

Her vehemence made Queenie laugh, and Hyde smiled too. He looked across at Queenie with open affection, feeling a sudden surge of optimism.

'Well, we know that Conchita's cousin says he saw me one place, when there's a witness I was someplace else. It was definitely a well-bred man, about the same size and build as your cousin, who set the ambushes, and it was someone with the same name as your cousin who sold our stolen mules to the livery barn in El Paso,' he said.

Conchita's bright expression wilted. 'But Ramon's always been so kind to me.'

'You're his kin,' Queenie pointed out. 'Pat and Robson are *Anglos*.'

Hyde looked at Conchita. 'Did you ever talk to Ramon about our silver caravans?'

Her face coloured as she nodded miserably. 'He was saying you were reckless when you shot the rattlesnake at the mine. I wanted him to admire you, so I told him how you had planned the route to El Paso, and where you thought you might be attacked. I'm sorry,' she cried. 'I've known him always. I trust him like I trust my father. I never thought it would be wrong to tell him when you were taking the silver to El Paso.'

'Don't blame yourself,' Queenie said warmly, reaching out to touch Conchita's arm. 'You couldn't know what he was planning.'

'Maybe it wasn't him,' Conchita said, trying to convince herself as much as the others. 'Ramon wouldn't bring shame on the family like that.'

Hyde stayed silent as Queenie spoke. 'From what Robson found in El Paso, it sounds as though Ramon must have been involved somehow. There would be too many coincidences, otherwise,' she said gently. 'And he did know the best places to set the ambushes.'

Conchita looked sorrowfully at Hyde, her eyes bright with unshed tears. '*Lo siento*. I'm sorry. I didn't mean to cause trouble.'

'Of course you didn't,' Hyde reassured her. 'You weren't to know your cousin would turn outlaw.' He leaned back in his chair and let out a long sigh.

'What are you going to do now?' Queenie asked.

Hyde took a bite of cheese as he thought. 'I surely have to speak to Pat first,' he decided. 'Tell him what I've found out, and what you've told me. We need to clear this up. Then we can talk to Ramon together, and get the truth.' He took a piece of bread. 'I need something to eat first though, I've been on the trail all day.'

Conchita clapped her hands for a servant.

'Do you want me to come with you?' she asked. 'I can tell Pat what I've just told you.'

Hyde shook his head. 'No thanks. This is between me and him.' He smiled at the two women. 'I reckon we'll all be glad when this mess is fixed.'

★   ★   ★

Ramon stealthily withdrew from the edge of the courtyard, where he'd been hidden from the group at the table by a rose-covered trellis. He hadn't intended

201

to eavesdrop, he'd simply intended to join Conchita and Señorita Williams at their table. But he'd heard an *Anglo* man's voice as he approached, and had closed in surreptitiously to listen. He'd heard most of the conversation, and was silently fuming as he moved away, still careful not to let the high heels of his boots clatter on the stone flags. Once back in the hacienda, he hurried towards the stables. He needed to find Vargas as quickly as possible.

His guess was right: Vargas was in the dirty cantina in Hueco, idly rolling a couple of dice on the table as he drank beer and eyed up the serving girls. Ramon stopped by his chair and bent to speak into his ear.

'We need to talk — outside.'

Vargas's deep-set eyes glared with resentment at being addressed so abruptly. 'I'm comfortable here,' he declared, leaning back into the wooden chair.

Ramon forgot his usual fear of his cousin's uncertain temper, and grabbed his arm to haul him up.

'I'm serious. This is urgent.'

Vargas snatched his arm from Ramon's grip, but stood. There was a mocking respect in his face as he looked at his slender cousin. He nodded, and pushed Ramon towards the rear door, following behind.

Once they were outside, Ramon glanced about to ensure that they wouldn't be overheard. Keeping his voice low, he told Vargas of the situation.

'Hyde's been to El Paso, and is at Don Pedro's hacienda now, talking to Conchita and one of Williams's sisters. He's worked out that it was me who took the silver, and he's got enough proof to convince the women. He's going to talk to Williams, and once he does, it's all up for us.'

'So what do you think we should do?' Vargas challenged him, his eyes sparkling with malicious glee.

'Hyde and Williams could get us sent to jail for a long time,' Ramon answered. 'Even if the jury aren't all *Anglos*, the judge will be, and he'll believe *Anglo* mine owners before he believes us. Without them, there will be no case. We have to kill them, and do it now.'

'You said Hyde was talking to Conchita and William's sister about the robberies. Do we kill them too?' Vargas asked coolly.

Ramon shook his head. 'No, not unless . . . We just threaten them, but if they are difficult, we may have to hurt Williams's sister.'

'They are just women,' Vargas remarked. 'They're not going to fight back against men. A few slaps should keep them in line.' He grinned recklessly at Ramon, his good spirits restored. 'We'll need backup. There are a couple of useful men in town. I'll round them up and meet you at the livery barn.' He laughed. 'I can get hold of something that will flush them out of wherever they're hiding.'

Ramon stared anxiously at him. 'You have dynamite?'

Vargas slapped Ramon heartily on the shoulder. 'Just a couple of sticks and the things to make them explode.'

'Have you ever used dynamite?' Ramon persisted.

Vargas stared, daring Ramon to contradict him. 'Yes, I've been shown how to fit the detonator caps and fuse. I don't intend to get my hand blown off — I've got too many uses for my right hand,' he added with a leer.

Ramon barely concealed his feeling of disgust. 'Then go get what you need. I want this over and done.'

★　★　★

Balzar came running to take Hyde's horse as usual when he reached the mine, but the young man had a skittish look to him.

'*Dónde está Señor Williams?*' Hyde asked.

Balzar didn't answer verbally, but turned worried eyes on the office building. Hyde thanked him, and headed that way.

On the ride from the hacienda he'd been thinking about Ramon, and marshalling his evidence, ready to put it to Pat Williams. Last year he'd come close to betraying Williams, but his partner had never suspected a thing. It had been Pat's trust and friendship that had stopped him from betraying himself and eventually running out. Right now, however, his conscience was clear. If Ramon's rumour-mongering had worried Pat at all, Hyde was confident it would easily be dealt with.

He pushed the door open and walked straight in. Williams was standing in front of the desk, his attention already on the door as Hyde entered. Hyde started to smile when he saw his friend, then saw the expression on Williams's face. There was no sign of the usual good nature, the blue eyes lacked their usual bright sparkle. Instead, Williams looked pinched and edgy. As Hyde came closer, Williams raised the right hand that had been hidden from view.

In a fast, smooth move, he brought his old revolver in line with Hyde's chest, the hammer cocked back and his finger firm on the trigger. Hyde froze, forcing himself to act calm.

'Have you betrayed me?' Williams asked, his voice ragged. 'Have *you* betrayed *me?*'

13

Hyde took a slow deep breath. Every muscle in his body was taut, the nerves screaming at him to take action, to defend himself. The cheap Colt copy held barely four feet from his chest looked like the most dangerous thing he'd ever faced. He made himself ignore it, and looked Williams in the face instead.

'No, Pat. Ramon has been telling lies,' he drawled.

The gun remained rock-steady in Williams's hand. 'He said you want to be rich again, like before the war. You want the mine for yourself. If I lose the mine, I'll lose Conchita. I'll lose everything.'

Hyde knew that all too well; he'd wrestled with that thought back when he had wanted the mine, a year ago. The memory of how he'd behaved back then sat uneasily on his conscience. The old guilt must have shown on his face, for Williams jerked the gun slightly, a bitter certainty in his eyes.

'You have been lying to me!' he accused.

'No!' Hyde flung back, knowing that right now he was in the clear.

'It's in your eyes. You've lied to me. Where did you go that day you went out for a long ride on your own? You never told me what you were doing,' Williams insisted.

This wasn't the way Hyde had wanted to discuss it, but he had no choice. Having no idea what Williams's reaction would be, he confessed.

'I was out riding with your sister, Queenie.'

Williams' eyes widened and Hyde believed for a moment that he was about to pull the trigger. His fingers twitched, ready to reach for his own guns.

'You're naming my sister as your alibi?' Williams said hoarsely.

'I was with her, and that's God's truth,' Hyde answered, his eyes drawn again to the gun aimed at his heart. 'That's what I've been lying about, Pat. I love Queenie, I keep thinking about her and I want to be with her.' The words began to spill out of him as he looked at his friend. 'Queenie cares about me, too. I know I should have spoken to you about her, but I didn't know if you'd take to having me court your sister. I reckoned it could wait until we'd fixed the problem of the robberies, and I guess I was putting it off, just because I didn't want to hear you say 'no'.'

Williams shook his head abruptly, as though trying to clear it. 'You've been lying about Queenie?' he questioned. 'Not telling me you've been seeing her, and that's why you've been acting odd?'

'Talk to Queenie,' Hyde said simply. He waited silently as Williams tried to take in this revelation. After a few moments, Williams's expression focused again.

'What about the stolen silver?' he asked. 'I saw it all stacked in the cave.

Someone was telling when and where to rob us.'

Acutely aware of the gun still pointed at him, Hyde tactfully explained how Conchita had told Ramon about the silver caravans, and how he'd discovered that Ramon had sold their stolen mules in El Paso. Williams listened intently, weighing up the arguments.

'There's one other thing,' Hyde added. The gun was still pointed at him, but Pat was listening and he was beginning to relax. 'The silver's been hidden in a cave, hasn't it?'

'That's so,' Williams agreed neutrally.

'Conchita said you had to go right in to find the silver cave. It took a minute or so to get to the cavern, following passages in the rock. She and Ramon both knew the area because they used to play there.'

When Williams nodded, Hyde continued: 'I hate going underground, Pat. You *know* that. I'd rather dig a hole and bury something than hide it underground.'

Williams blinked. 'You're right,' he said slowly. 'You'd hate going to that cavern.' To Hyde's silent relief, William's arm began to relax, the gun pointing towards the corner.

Absorbed in their confrontation, neither man had taken much notice of sounds from outside. Hyde had been distantly aware of his horse whinnying and snorting in the nearby corral, but his attention had been fully focused on Williams. Now, as he took a deep breath, he was more conscious of the sound of his horse calling to another. He turned his head to the sound, and as he did, something came flying in through the open window at the side of the office. Both Williams and Hyde watched as it landed on the floor near the back of the room, between themselves and their bedrooms. Simultaneously, they registered that it was two sticks of dynamite, lashed together, with a burning cord attached.

If it had exploded within the next second or two, both men would have been badly hurt. But for all his confident talk to Ramon, Vargas had made the cord slightly too long. A single glance was enough to tell Hyde and Williams that they had a few seconds to react. Both raced for the office door, Hyde drawing his matched guns as he moved.

'Open for me!' he barked.

Williams didn't argue; as Hyde moved to one side, he grabbed the handle with his free hand and yanked the door open. Hyde was diving through even as it opened. Williams followed, hearing the crash of gunfire as he went the other way. They had barely got outside when the dynamite exploded. Williams felt the blast on his back, flinging him further forward.

A couple of shots went somewhere over Hyde's body as he hit the ground on his side and rolled, coming up onto his knees. He saw five men, one of them Ramon, and all armed. His guns aimed almost of their own accord; he fired, and one of the men pitched backwards as a bullet tore through his chest. A shot cracked past Hyde's head, and he returned fire. Another man staggered and dropped to one knee, but kept hold of his gun. Lunging to his feet, Hyde fired both guns as he sprinted for the two trees between the office building and the corral. One of his attackers flinched and backed away, but a sturdy, barrel-shaped man raced towards him, his face alive with the joy of the fight.

Williams landed belly down, his back stinging from the blast. The force of the impact jolted his gun loose from his hand, and it skittered a couple of feet further on. Stunned, Williams could do nothing but lie where he'd landed and gasp for breath. He could hear shots and a scream of pain; the seconds it took for him to pull himself together seemed a very long time. Forcing himself into action, Williams managed to heave himself onto hands and knees.

'Williams!'

Hearing the shout, he turned and found Ramon just a few feet away, his face alight with triumph as he aimed his revolver squarely at Williams's head.

Gunfire crackled around Hyde as he ran. He felt a sharp tug on one side of his gunbelt, and knew a bullet had struck it. Spinning, he found himself facing three men. Two had guns, one of them being the man he'd wounded. The heavyset third, Vargas, was running towards him with a knife in either hand. Another shot cracked past as he lunged to one side and fired both guns in return. One shot missed, but the kneeling man screamed thinly and folded over, clutching at his belly. Hyde's brain was working at lightning speed, calculating distance and time between opponents.

Smoothly, he twisted sideways, firing again before the remaining gunman could get a shot off. The gunman lurched backwards, hit in the shoulder, and valiantly tried to realign his revolver in Hyde's direction. Hyde took a moment longer to aim, and shot him in the head. As the gunman buckled and collapsed, Hyde turned his attention to Vargas. He was almost too late.

Vargas was still some ten feet away, but the knife in his left hand was a throwing knife. As Hyde turned to him, he was sweeping his arm forward in a throw. Hyde frantically twisted, instinctively throwing up his left arm to try and block the flying knife with his gun. The knife sliced across the back of his hand and through the top of his shoulder. Hyde let out a hiss of pain, and tried to bring his guns to bear, but Vargas was barrelling into him, his Bowie knife slashing for Hyde's belly. Hyde just managed to bring his hands together, crossing them at the wrists. He blocked Vargas's knife slash and twisted, deflecting it to one side, but Vargas was coming on at full tilt. Vargas slammed into Hyde and the two of them tumbled backwards, Hyde underneath as they hit the ground.

Williams dropped into a sitting position as he looked up at Ramon, standing as straight and tall as he could.

'If you kill me, Conchita will never forgive you,' Williams said in Spanish.

Ramon snorted. 'She is young. She will forget the *Anglo* dog she thought she loved.'

'She does love me,' Williams insisted.

'Concepción is a lady from one of the oldest and noblest families in Texas,' Ramon replied proudly. 'She should marry one like herself, not *you*.'

'Don Pedro thinks I'm good enough. What's good enough for him should be good enough for you.'

'No.' Ramon shook his head. 'If you didn't have the silver mine, he would never consider you. He would be looking for a good Spanish husband for her. That's what he should have done anyway, instead of letting your money win him over.'

Williams hid his anger at Ramon's verdict on his worth. Instead, he answered back: 'I suppose *you* think you're the ideal *criollo* for her? Wouldn't you like to be the *terrateniente* at Casa de las Flores, and have

Conchita as your wife? That's what you care about. You don't care if you have to hurt her to get it.'

While sitting up, Williams had managed to put his right hand over a stone. His pistol was just out of reach, but the stone was concealed in his palm. He was talking in an effort to distract Ramon and get him to drop his aim, just for a moment.

Ramon scowled. 'I do care about Conchita. That's why I want what's best for her, and an upstart *Anglo* of no family, like you, is not best for Doña Concepción Maria Flores de la Valle. You are not fit to wipe her shoes,' he went on, years of bitterness at *Anglos* spilling out of him. 'You are not fit to speak to her.'

Williams heard a shout from behind, and the bark of a rifle. Ramon flinched, looking past Williams towards the bunkhouse. His gun lifted, aiming towards whoever had started shooting from the bunkhouse. Williams took his chance, and flung the stone as hard as he could. As soon as it left his hand, he dived sideways, grabbing for his gun. The stone struck Ramon's face, just below the eye. He screamed in anger and pain, recoiling from the blow. Williams got his hand on his gun and whipped it round, recklessly fanning the hammer. Blue gunsmoke coiled around him as he fired four rapid shots in Ramon's direction. Half-deafened by his own gunfire, Williams couldn't tell if Ramon had fired back at him. His tense body anticipated the agony of a bullet, but through the billows of gunpowder, he made out Ramon's shape staggering and falling. Williams rolled and scrambled to his feet, his gun still aimed in Ramon's direction.

Ramon was lying on his back, his handsome face twisted in pain, Scarlet blood bubbled from bullet wounds in his chest as he struggled to breathe. He turned his head slowly, glaring at Williams, then his eyes lost focus. His head rolled to one side, his limbs twitching randomly as he died. After a few more moments he lay completely still, his eyes empty. Williams let out a sudden sigh of relief.

Hyde dropped his guns as he hit the ground, grabbing for Vargas's knife arm. He seized the wrist, holding Vargas's arm at full stretch. The heavyset man had landed atop him, bringing their faces close enough for Hyde to smell Vargas's breath. Although Vargas was the heavier, Hyde used his long arms to keep Vargas's knife arm locked straight and out to one side. Vargas didn't waste time trying to pull himself loose; he simply used his free hand to punch Hyde in the stomach.

Vargas didn't have the room to use his full strength, but the impact was enough to make Hyde lose his breath in an explosive gasp. The blow weakened Hyde long enough for Vargas to break the lock. He brought the Bowie knife back across, aiming for Hyde's face. Hyde still had a hold of Vargas's wrist, even though he no longer had full control. As the blade slashed at him, he turned his face away and frantically pushed Vargas's hand upwards. He felt a sting across his cheekbone, but he'd managed to raise the blade enough for it to make only a shallow cut across his face, instead of slicing to the bone. Hyde tightened his grip on the wrist again and pushed Vargas's hand further in the direction it was already moving. With the help of one foot braced against the ground, he rolled in the direction he'd pushed, throwing Vargas off, and rolling on top of him in turn.

He pushed himself up, so he was kneeling astride the other man, and tried to force the knife down towards Vargas's throat. Hyde could feel warm blood sliding across his face from the knife wound. They struggled for a moment, Hyde trying to use his weight to overcome Vargas's greater strength. For a moment, their eyes met. Hyde saw no fear or anger, just the gleam of challenge at their kill-or-be-killed struggle. Then Vargas suddenly stopped resisting the pressure. Hyde was taken by surprise, and although he forced the arm down, Vargas managed to twist it enough that it slammed harmlessly into the dirt by his side. Hyde lurched forward slightly, and Vargas used the moment to take a jab at Hyde's groin.

Hyde glimpsed just enough of the blow to tell where it was aimed. He twisted his hips, pulling himself back at the same time. Vargas's fist hit his thigh first, then slid to hit Hyde's crotch. Hyde gasped as pain shot through the sensitive area, and momentarily lost focus. Vargas bucked his body upwards, trying to dislodge Hyde. However, Hyde had sat many a bucking horse, and he instinctively tightened the grip with his legs, and adjusted his balance. As he moved his legs in, he felt his right spur touch Vargas's leg. As Vargas attempted to jerk his knife hand free, Hyde twisted his feet outwards, and slammed his spurs into Vargas's thighs.

Vargas yelled at the unexpected pain, his body tensing.

'Take it, you son-of-a-bitch,' Hyde

snarled as blood from the knife cut ran into the corner of his mouth. Putting his free hand on Vargas's chest for balance, he slammed his spurs into Vargas's legs again, and straightened his legs, dragging his spurs brutally along the other man's thighs as he did so.

Vargas bit back the cry of pain and instead made a violent effort to throw Hyde off. As he convulsed, he lifted his knife hand away from the ground. Hyde saw his opportunity. Grabbing Vargas's wrist with both hands, he got control of the knife for long enough to thrust it down into Vargas's neck. Blood squirted up from around the blade as Vargas tried frantically to dislodge Hyde. Bubbles of blood foamed at his mouth and nose as he fought for air. Ruthlessly, Hyde twisted the blade, making the wound larger.

Vargas gasped incoherent obscenities in Spanish, almost snarling in his rage at his killer. Hyde let go his grip of Vargas's wrist and sat more upright, chilled by the sight of the furious, dying man. Vargas made a couple of feeble attempts to pluck the knife from his throat, but his hand dropped as weakness overtook him. The curses faded as he began to choke and cough on his blood. The look of resentful anger stayed in his deep-set eyes until just moments before they closed for the last time.

'You got what you no doubt thoroughly deserved,' Hyde drawled quietly. Then, suddenly remembering Williams, he forced himself to his feet and turned to see what had happened.

Williams was standing, and speaking to O'Reilly, Goras, Banderas and Busby, who had all emerged from the bunkhouse with guns. Williams slapped Banderas on the shoulder, thanking him. Hyde walked over to join the group, and saw Ramon's body stretched out on the ground. The group around Williams dispersed, some checking the bodies, while Goras headed for the corral.

'You all right?' Hyde asked.

'Back's a mite sore,' Williams replied,

gingerly working his shoulders. 'You look like you could use some fixing up.'

Hyde pulled a crumpled handkerchief from his jacket pocket and wiped blood from his face. 'Could have been worse.'

'I'm sending Goras to Don Pedro. He'll want to see the bodies and identify Ramon.' Williams paused, glanced at the body and sighed, before continuing. 'I'll ask him to send someone who's good at stitching wounds.' He paused again, gazing at the ground for a few moments before looking at his friend.

'I can't say how sorry I am that I doubted you,' Williams said. 'I guess I was just so frightened at the thought of losing Conchita that I wanted someone to blame, and Ramon offered someone.'

'A man will do crazy things to protect what's important to him,' Hyde drawled.

Williams nodded. 'Ramon was trying to protect Conchita from the *Anglos* he hated. I think the silver was secondary to him.'

'Not to me it isn't,' Hyde said, so

forthrightly that Williams smiled.

'Come on,' he said. 'Let's go start getting you fixed up. You got to look presentable when you next see Queenie.'

Hyde hesitated a moment, then grinned. 'You're happy for me to court Queenie?'

'There's no one I'd trust more with my sister than my partner,' Williams said. 'Besides, I always reckoned that Queenie had the most sense of any of my sisters, so I'm not arguing with her choice. And it's my duty to see that she gets her man with as little damage as possible.'

With that, he gave Hyde a gentle nudge in the direction of the bunkhouse.

★　★　★

Williams arranged to have the bodies laid out neatly and covered by blankets, which was as well, because Don Pedro arrived with Conchita and Queenie, as well as some of his men and a wagon.

As soon as she saw Williams, Conchita slithered from her saddle without waiting for help, and ran to him.

'Pat! Oh, I'm so sorry. If I hadn't told Ramon about your silver caravans, he might not have been tempted.'

Williams took hold of her hands and gazed into her shining eyes.

'Please don't blame yourself, sweetheart. When someone is as determined as Ramon was, they will find a way.'

Don Pedro had dismounted with more dignity, and followed his daughter over to Williams. The bulky, powerful man offered his hand.

'I am truly sorry that, once again, an individual has brought shame on my family by his actions towards you,' he said.

'I am certain that you had nothing to do with Ramon's actions,' Williams replied formally. 'And that you would have stopped him if you knew.'

Don Pedro nodded. 'I deeply regret what has happened and I am glad you are not seriously injured. Unfortunately, Ramon's family home was taken by *Anglo* settlers when he was a very young child. He had long harboured a grudge against *Anglos.*'

'And the thought of one marrying Conchita was too much for him,' Williams said, glancing at his lovely fiancée.

'Yes,' Don Pedro remarked. 'I was talking to Conchita on the way here. Although I pray that no one else will attempt to harm you in any way, I think it better that you should be married sooner rather than later. Once you are Conchita's husband, and part of my family, your position will be more secure. I suggest that you be married before the year is out.'

Pat Williams had been expecting his engagement to last for at least a year, so Don Pedro's suggestion was a surprise, but a welcome one. He grinned, and looked again at Conchita, who was smiling too.

'I reckon that's a swell idea,' he said warmly, and turned to look for his friend.

Hyde had helped Queenie down from her saddle. She looked at him anxiously, raising her gloved fingers to the barely hardened scab on his cheek, without actually touching it.

'Don Pedro brought an old woman who's good with wounds,' she said. 'I'll get her to work on you right away.'

'Looking at you is all the medicine I need right now,' Hyde drawled, gazing contentedly at her.

Queenie hesitated a moment, distracted from her concern, then smiled radiantly. Hyde took her hand, and they stayed that way, content in simply being with one another.

'Queenie. Hyde.' Williams's call interrupted their spell.

Looking around, Hyde saw Williams with Conchita by his side, her arm through his. Williams was grinning, and Conchita was openly happy.

'Don Pedro reckons as we should get married this year,' Williams announced, squeezing Conchita's arm gently. 'And that being so, I reckon as how you two should wait until next year for your wedding.'

Hyde turned to Queenie. 'I think I just proposed to you.'

Queenie smiled. 'You can ask me properly sometime when we're alone. But the answer will be 'yes'.'

And in spite of his tiredness, and the sting of his knife wounds, Hyde smiled.

THE END

LANIGAN AND THE SHE-WOLF

Ronald Martin Wade

Silas Cutler hires Shawnee Lanigan to track down the bank robbers who abducted his eighteen-year-old daughter, Sara Beth. The ruthless 'La Loba' leads the all female gang. When he tracks the outlaws down, he's staggered to discover the real reason for the kidnapping ... Forced to report his failed rescue mission, he takes work supervising security for a mining operation. Lanigan unveils a plot and ultimately faces a vengeful mob — aware that they can't all make it out alive ...

SHARPSHOOTER McCLURE

I. J. Parnham

US Marshal Jesse Cole sends deputy sheriff Mick McClure to infiltrate the hired guns harassing the homesteaders of Harmony. But a night of bloody carnage ends in failure with the marshal dead. Mike escap es but, trailed by the gunslingers, Mike assumes a new identity, working with Brandon Webb's Wild West Show. However, memories of that terrible night ensure his return to Harmony. He'll need all his gun skills to bring the guilty parties to justice.

LONG SHADOWS

Terry James

When Jake Rudd is saved from a beating by an old flame, his plans to settle down seem a possibility. Unfortunately, Ros West doesn't remember him, and with trouble following her there's no reason to trust him. Only when a power-hungry businessman threatens family and friends, does the past bring events full circle. Together, Jake and Ros must deal with the past to secure the future, even though the truth could be more dangerous than a smoking gun . . .